Sacher-Masoch, Emma M. Phelps

Seraph

A Tale of Hungary

Sacher-Masoch, Emma M. Phelps

Seraph
A Tale of Hungary

ISBN/EAN: 9783743444232

Printed in Europe, USA, Canada, Australia, Japan

Cover: Foto ©Andreas Hilbeck / pixelio.de

More available books at **www.hansebooks.com**

SERAPII.

A TALE OF HUNGARY.

BY

SACHER-MASOCH.

TRANSLATED BY

EMMA M. PHELPS.

NEW YORK:

GEO. M. ALLEN COMPANY,

BROADWAY, CORNER 21ST STREET.

SERAPH.

CHAPTER I.

Ein Juengling wie ein Mann.—LESSING.

SHOOT!" exclaimed Stefanida, springing up from the chair where she had been sitting, and holding high up in one hand a card with the ace of hearts painted on it. "Shoot! that all here may see I have spoken the truth."

The circle of guests gathered around the fire, peacefully engaged in drinking tea, was thrown into a state of great perturbation by these words of their hostess.

"Jesus—Mary—Joseph!" bleated out an old lady seated in the chair nearest the fire, and seemed about to fall from her seat in a swoon.

"What nonsense is this!" exclaimed Pan * Kostezki, taking a huge pinch out of his

---

*Hungarian title answering to Sir or Mr.

jewelled snuff-box, and holding it up to his nose in the vain attempt to conceal that he, even he, an old officer under Napoleon, had turned pale.

"It is not nonsense at all," returned Madame Temkin, turning angrily toward him; then addressing her son, she continued: "Get your pistol, Seraph, I beg of you."

The young man to whom these words were spoken got up from the chair where he had been seated and came forward. A tall, handsome youth he stood there before his mother, his head slightly bent, as though awaiting her commands. A slight flush was on his face; his blue eyes, usually so dreamy, flashed brightly.

"Will you shoot?" his mother asked impatiently.

"At your command," he answered promptly. He went to the chimney-piece and took down his pistols which hung there above it.

"You see, Pan Kostezki," said Stefanida, a touch of scorn curving her full red lips, "you see my son is not willing his mother should lie under an imputation of having told a falsehood."

"A thousand pardons, gracious lady," stammered the little old man, burying his sharp chin still deeper within the folds of his broad white neckcloth, "but who has accused you of such a thing? Certainly not I. I simply related a story of a nobleman living in the last century who, as a pastime, often shot the high heels off his wife's velvet slippers when those same slippers were on madame's dainty little feet. And she, in her turn, would loose the buckles of his belt with a bullet from her pistol——"

"Quite true," Madame Temkin interrupted him; "and when I, in return, said that my Seraph was even a better marksman than that lord and his lady, you smiled incredulously."

"I smiled, and incredulously!" murmured the horrified old man. "How could I dream of doubting anything that a lady I esteem so highly—a lady——"

"You did smile, and scornfully!"

"But, gracious lady, what a dilemma you put me in! How can I acknowledge I was rude enough to smile incredulously at anything a lady might say?—and if I deny I smiled, I contradict a lady. Which is worse? You must decide for yourself."

"You know you are a wicked old sceptic," returned his hostess laughingly. "You were born a sceptic and brought up in the ideas of Voltaire and the French Revolution. You really only believe in two things—in the great Napoleon and in the Cossack who wounded you in the arm by a sabre-thrust at Grochow."

"Alas! in the Cossack I must perforce believe."

"You are only to be convinced by material evidence, by what you can see and hear and feel, and that is why I insist on Seraph's shooting the ace out of this card immediately while I hold it up for him."

"Very well," returned Pan Kostezki, rising from his chair, "let him shoot the ace out of the card if you choose, but you must not hold it for him; we will pin it here on a panel of the door."

"No, I shall hold it for him. I—myself."

"Pray, do not think of doing anything so rash—so foolhardy!"

"We cannot allow you to risk your life in that way."

"Why attempt a thing so rash?"

"It is tempting God to do it," resounded from all sides of the room. And at the same time the ladies present surrounded Madame Temkin and endeavored to take the card away from her.

"I am risking nothing," she returned, breaking away from them. "I know my son and what he can do. Not a hair of my head will be injured."

"And you really have the courage?"

"Oh, in this case," returned Stefanida, "it requires more courage to shoot than to be shot at. Come, Seraph, show that you are a man."

"I really cannot consent to it, as I was unfortunately the innocent cause——"

"Please, all of you, draw aside," commanded the hostess, "that my son's aim may not be impeded."

Seraph, placing himself against the wall opposite and raising his pistol, took aim with it. The ladies of the company cowered in the deep recesses of the windows, while Stefanida, leaning lightly against a small table, a smile of contempt playing about her full red lips, held the card above her head in one small jewelled hand. Her eyes were fastened calmly and proudly on her son. A moment of suspense—of breathless expectation. A flash, followed by a report; then a loud clapping of hands by the spectators. Madame Temkin held the card up triumphantly. The ace had been shot clean out of it. While all surrounded the hostess with congratulations on her son's skill, Seraph, as if awaking from slumber, pushed his thick blond hair slowly off his forehead. On him, as he stood there half-unconscious of what was passing around him, rested half-admiringly, half-mockingly, a pair of blue eyes belonging to a young and slender woman, who, with her small feet buried in a white wolf-skin rug, was seated on a low chair before the fire. Her intent gaze caused him to turn toward her. A slight movement of her haughty little head, a dimpling mischievous smile drew him to her side. She leaned back upon the cushions and, throwing back her head, looked up at him as he stood there behind her chair.

"Do you know I am almost in love with you to-night, Seraph?" she said laughingly, holding out a little trembling hand toward him.

He stooped and kissed the slender hand. "You?" he retorted, smiling doubtfully.

"Yes—I. After all, I think I have always been a little in love with you all my life long, really."

"What new caprice is this of yours, Barbara?"

"If you are in such an inaccessible humor, I must ask you, monsieur, to call me 'gracious lady' as the others do."

"As you please, Madame Trendaloska," Seraph returned, bowing deeply.

She sprang up from her seat quickly, and

catching hold of his bent-down head she pulled his blond hair rudely—the action of a naughty, ill-bred child.

"You have learned nothing sensible out of those dry, thick tomes you are always poring over. / I must give you some lessons. I will be your school-mistress." And as she stood there before him, her tall, slender figure drawn up to its full height, the thick ash-blond hair combed off her low, white forehead, her blue eyes sparkling brightly from beneath slender, black, level brows, her full lips parted over her small, white teeth, she was indeed a school-mistress that even the most headstrong and stubborn pupil would have found it easy to obey.

"It is time for me to take my leave," she continued, after a pause; then turning to Madame Temkin, "I may take Seraph home with me, may I not?"

"Certainly," was the answer. "Have Barbara's horse brought round, and order yours to be saddled also."

Seraph shook his head gently.

"What, you refuse to accompany me?" exclaimed Madame Trendaloska angrily.

A reproving glance from his mother caused her son to give way, while a gentle pressure of her hand calmed Barbara's rising anger.

The other guests had risen and were making their adieux to the hostess. When the last carriage had driven off Seraph lifted Madame Trendaloska into her saddle, then mounted his own horse, which a groom was holding by the bridle.

"Good-night," they cried, kissing their hands to Madame Temkin, who stood watching their departure from the window. A fresh spring breeze was blowing from across the steppes. Everything upon Barbara was waving and fluttering in this wind—the veil around her hat, the long skirt of her habit, even a long blond braid of her hair which had come unloosed and fallen down upon her shoulders.

The moon had a white turban of clouds around her head when they started, but the frolicsome wind soon tore it off, and the soft light streamed down over the landscape.

The river rushed madly on, the slender pollards on its banks swaying to and fro in elfin-like dance. The white clouds in the sky were driven furiously onward by the wind, like a flock of lambs pursued by wolves. The weathercock on the tall church tower, silvered by the moonbeams, creaked and groaned hoarsely. They galloped on through the sleeping village, and turning into a small park drew up before a low, broad house, half hidden by tall sentinel trees. Seraph swung himself off his horse, and lifting Madame Trendaloska from the saddle, he raised his hat in adieu and was about to remount, when she exclaimed:

"No, Seraph, you must not go yet; come into the house with me."

They passed through the door which a sleepy servant held open for them, and walked down the long corridor into the drawing-room, out of which Barbara's boudoir opened.

She hurried away to take off her habit, returning, however, so quickly that Seraph had hardly time to realize that he might

have escaped had he chosen to do so. She
had changed her habit for a *peignoir* of
sea-green silk, heavily trimmed with Valen-
ciennes lace. She nodded smilingly to Seraph as she sank down lazily into the cush-
ioned depths of an arm-chair. At this
moment her beauty, in the dim, soft lights
of the pink-shaded lamps, was quite daz-
zling. It seemed to Seraph as if he and his
companion in this small, dainty perfumed
apartment, where there was hardly room
enough for them to turn around, were shut
up together in a huge *bonbonnière*. He felt
half suffocated in the heavy perfumed at-
mosphere after the sweet, fresh air outside.
With a sudden impatient movement he
pushed back his chair. She looked at him
curiously, half shrugged her shoulders, then
springing from her chair, she went to a
mirror hanging opposite and, taking up an
open jewel-casket lying on the table in
front of it, began bedecking herself with
its contents. She thrust a long gold pin
through the ash-blond braids of her hair,
hung a pair of ear-rings in her small pink

ears, fastened a broad jewelled collar round her white throat, and drew bracelet after bracelet over her slender wrists and round arms. To finish all, she put on over her shoulders a jacket of scarlet velvet lined and bordered with sable which was hanging across the screen. She was now fairly glittering with gold and precious stones like an image of a Madonna in some old Russian shrine. "Do you like me better now?" she cried laughingly. "Am I gorgeous and glittering enough to suit you?" Like the perfect coquette that she was, Madame Trendaloska was well aware what charms she possessed and what she lacked. She had been brought up by her father, who had educated her like the son he had desired her to be. To this training she owed her health, her fresh, bright coloring, her absolute fearlessness, but it had in a measure robbed her of woman's soft grace and subtle charm. The lustre of velvet and satin, the softness of clinging fur, were necessary to her to cover a slight angularity of form and harshness of contour.

Seraph measured her as she stood there before him, with glances half approving, half critical. She did not resent the criticism, evidently, but with a sudden impetuous, almost childish movement she threw her arms around his neck.

"Will you not behave yourself as you should?" she asked with a pretty impatience. "Any other man in your place would be dying to fling himself at my feet. But you— you are an iceberg—a polar bear. Still you are very handsome, Seraph, provokingly, abominably handsome——"

"How long have you thought me so, pray?"

"Only since this evening," she replied promptly. She paused a moment and continued: "It is odd, but though we have been together, always together since I can remember, and have played and quarrelled and hated each other as children do, and grown up side by side, it has only just occurred to me that you have become a man, a charming, handsome man; and you on your part have been quite as obtuse—you have never noticed that I have grown to be a woman—a beautiful woman, whose right it is to demand and receive admiration, homage—love even."

"Oh, I loved you, Barbara—loved you from the time that you were only a half-grown girl running about in short frocks, and with your long plaits of hair hanging down on your shoulders. I loved you, and as a boy I determined to ask you to marry me when I was grown up; but then you see they married you to some one else before I *was* grown up."

"To a man I hate!"

Seraph shrugged his shoulders. "So much the worse for us both. But, as you can see for yourself, our romance must be laid aside, though we had only got beyond the first chapters."

"Our romance put aside unfinished," she returned eagerly; "why should we not go on with it, pray?"

"I am not the man to love a married woman."

"We shall see."

Seraph shook his head. This action of his enraged her so much that she sprang from her chair and, stamping her little foot violently, went on:

"You will fall in love with me! You shall! You shall be my slave, my abject slave—do you hear me?"

He smiled disdainfully and answered: "Do not force me to say something rude to you, Barbara."

She turned from him impatiently and began walking up and down the apartment struggling, but vainly, to conceal her anger. The short train of her gown whisked from side to side after her like the tail of some green, shining lizard.

"You are really vexed with me, Barbara?"

"Yes."

"Then I had better bid you good-night." He rose as he spoke and went toward the door.

"No, no, Seraph, do not leave me," she answered pleadingly, and barred his way. "Do not be so harsh to me. You love me, I am sure of it. Have you not just told me that you loved me—that you wished to marry me?" She caught hold of his hand and began stroking it gently. "Come! speak to me. Say one kind word to me, and at once! Do you hear, sir? What I want I must have at once. To-day I love you; to-morrow I may not, perhaps."

"You have so many adorers, Barbara. Every man who comes near you, like a moth round a candle, burns himself in the light of your beauty. What new folly is it of yours to fancy yourself in love with me?"

"I love you——"

"Caprice! pure caprice, on your part, Barbara."

"I shall weep when you have gone away from me."

"For the want of something better to do."

"Not so. I have a real affection for you, Seraph."

"And I for you. I am good enough for a friend, but not good at all for a lover—a slave. And you, you treat the men who love you like the cushion beneath your feet."

"Go," she muttered, turning angrily away from him. "Leave me."

"Good-night." But there was no reply to his salutation.

As he mounted his horse and rode rapidly out of the gate, he heard the sound of a window above him opening, but did not turn his head.

When the young man returned to Dirvin, the lights in the house were all extinguished except in the little drawing-room, where he found his mother seated before the fire, staring gloomily into the flames.

"Have you been waiting for me?" he exclaimed, throwing aside his hat and whip and kneeling down before her to kiss her hand.

"How gallant!" said Stefanida, with a slight, bitter smile. "But this act of homage belongs probably to the woman you have just left?"

"You think I find Barbara irresistible?"

"Why should you not?" his mother answered scornfully. "She is, perhaps, not beautiful according to the absurd rules of

2

art, which artists themselves despise, but she is lovely—she is fascinating—she is dangerous."

"Not to me."

"So much the better, my son, for you should certainly have a higher, a more serious aim in life than to play the rôle of Seladon to a married coquette." While speaking, she passed her hand half fondly, half absently over her son's fair hair, her gaze fixed on the red, leaping flames of the wood fire.

Stefanida was a woman still charming enough to hold a man captive by her charms. A young man, perhaps, more easily than one her senior.

She had come to an age when a woman in return for her girlish loveliness is endowed with a subtler, a more gracious and tender charm. Only really beautiful, however, were her great gray eyes, and her figure, which was quite perfect.

She had the shape of a Greek Venus, but her face was not Greek; its features were quite irregular, Calmuck almost, in character.

Her son knelt before her now, a grown
man, as he had knelt a child listening to the
strange, wild tales she was fond of telling
him by the light of the fire—the story of
Zarewitsch and the gaunt winged wolf, or
that of Iwanok the pitiless Jew; but there
was still another tale she had told him over
and over again—that never-to-be-forgotten
but only half-understood tale which haunted
his memory and tortured him; a story of
the man with a heart of stone, who had injured her and made her whole life wretched,
miserable.

Now she told it again, and her listener's
blood boiled in his veins as he knelt there
drinking down her words.

Deep silence succeeded the recital.

It was the hour when the silver gates
which shut us out from the unseen wonder-
land about us are opened.

Wind and fire spoke softly to each other,
the gnawing of the mouse behind the wain-
scot was plainly to be heard. The death-
watch ticked in the wall, the cricket chirped
on the hearth. The curtains before the win-

dows were transformed into tall, fluttering
white ghosts and whispered together softly.
The closets and presses creaked gloomily,
the small porcelain dancing-figures on the
chimney-piece seemed to swing and sway
gently to and fro. Outside the branches of
the tall trees held solemn converse with the
night-wind. The time-bleached portraits on
the wall glowed in the ruddy light of the
fire, and beneath them sat Madame Temkin,
motionless as they, with the firelight playing
on her hair and in her eyes, wrapped in the
dark fur of her jacket, her feet resting on a
black bear-skin rug. In the Rembrandtish
half-light she seemed herself a picture fresh
from the easel of some Slavonic artist. The
moonlight streaming through the window,
from whence the curtain had been drawn
back, had softened the expression of her
face, usually rather cruel, and tempered the
savage glitter in her dark gray eyes. And
the youth at her feet contemplated her
with glances of respectful admiration, unquestioning devotion—a gaze more suited
to a Madonna surrounded by a celestial

halo than to a living, every-day human being.

"It is really excellent," she began with an acid smile, "that you refuse to be drawn into the net so openly set for you by Barbara. Otherwise you would have been lost to me, for a time at least—not for always. You are not the man, I am glad to say, to wear long the shackles of a woman like Barbara. You may thank me for that. You owe to my rigid training your nerves of steel, your calm, cool temperament, your clear brain, your self-control, your habit of self-examination. You are a man now, young and strong, firm of will, and steadfast in character. You are no idle dreamer. You see and judge of things as they are. You know your place in the world and what you owe to it. You also know what it owes to you."

"And to you, mother, I have long known what I owe to you. You wish me to do something for you—to perform a task you have set for me. But what this task is I do not yet know."

"The time has come for you to know it."

"It has come. What has it brought with it for me to do?"

"Why have I, do you think, Seraph, educated you like a warrior of a past heroic age, had you trained like a Roman gladiator? Why have I insisted on your becoming an expert with the pistol and the sword?"

"I have often wondered why."

"Now you shall hear," returned his mother, bending down toward him with a quick movement, her fresh, bright face framed by the waves of her red-brown hair, her gray eyes darting flames no less brilliant than the fire's. "I have reared you like a Spartan youth that you might one day be my knight—the avenger of my wrongs."

"On whom am I to wreak this vengeance? On that man who used you so cruelly—injured you so deeply? But you have never yet explained to me how he injured you."

"Yes, on him. On him who used me as one uses a common flower of the steppes that catches one's eyes as one rides past; one plucks it up by the roots, carries it away

with one a mile or so, and when the poor
flower droops and fades, one flings it with
careless hand away. He who, when I like
an eagle would have soared aloft, broke my
wings. The man who disdained, deceived,
betrayed me. He who blasted my happiness, wasted my youth, destroyed my peace
and my faith in this world and my hope of
the next—Emilian Theodorowitsch."

"It is the first time that I have heard his
name."

"That I know well," his mother answered,
with a scornful curl of her lip. "He does
not live here, but in another part of the
country—a long way from here. He lives
among the mountains on the edge of a ravine; a place fit only for owls to nest in.
He has hidden himself from the world—from
me—as he has good reason to do."

Seraph sighed heavily.

"Why do you not answer me?" asked his
mother impatiently. "Have you nothing to
say to me?"

"This man whose name I hear now for
the first time——"

"Theodorowitsch."

"Has he indeed injured you so deeply, mother, that you cannot forgive him?"

"Forgive *him?* Never!"

"Do you think revenge can make one happy? Can one regain a lost happiness by destroying the happiness, the peace of another? To kill, to take the life even of an enemy—can it be a pleasure? I do not think so."

"I know better than you what will give me pleasure," his mother answered him, darkly frowning. "I know that I should taste happiness—pure and unalloyed happiness—if I could in one moment, in the twinkling of an eye, rob him of all which he holds dear in this world. Yes, I should be unspeakably happy could I see him at this very moment writhing out his life at my feet."

"Mother, such feelings as those are quite unknown, incomprehensible to me."

"They are wicked, dreadful feelings, those of mine, you would tell me. It may be so, but with tender sentiments, lofty aims, one cannot battle with life, with the world. Sooner or later one must draw off one's gloves and with hard, bare fists strike about one."

"Possibly; but to fight—that is better than to injure wantonly—to revenge."

"I only know what I wish done, what will give me peace after intolerable pain."

"Mother," returned Seraph gravely, "have you reflected calmly on the task you would give me?⁄ 'Man fires the rifle, but God it is who sends the bullet on its way,' is a saying, you know, of our peasants. Tell me at least, and plainly, what they are, your secret wrongs, your hidden sufferings, and let me judge for myself what I should do. No, not judge, but decide with the heart of a son, of a devoted, loving son, if it would not be best for you to forgive the injury you have received, the wrongs you have suffered."

"It would take too long," Stefanida returned impatiently. "I ask, I demand from you the obedience, the utter and unquestioning obedience that a child owes to its parent."

"What is it, then, you require of me?"

She hesitated. She gave her son a long, searching look, while her fingers fumbled nervously with the fur trimming of her jacket.

"I beseech you," said Seraph, rising, "put an end to this. Tell me what it is you wish me to do."

"You—must—kill—him." she answered, half under her breath.

"I—kill— No, mother, that I cannot do. You ask too much."

"I command you to do so, and you will obey me."

"No, mother, never will I become an assassin—a cold-blooded murderer. You ask too much, I say."

"Who ever asked that of you?"

"I do not understand," returned the young man wearily, "what it is you want me to do."

"I wish you to challenge him, to fight a duel with him. You two will fight, and you will kill him, I am sure of it."

"A duel! but how—when—where is it

to be fought?" asked Seraph, walking impatiently up and down the room.

"Promise me."

"What?"

"Give me your hand upon it, that you will obey me—blindly obey me."

Stefanida got up out of the chair where she had been sitting and came toward her son, her bright gray eyes fixed sternly upon him. She held out her hand toward him with a gesture full of command.

He took it trembling.

"I will, mother," he said reluctantly, "though an inward voice warns me to beware."

"I thank you, my son," she replied, drawing a long, deep sigh of satisfaction. "And now go you to bed. It is late, and to-morrow—or rather to-day, for look, the dawn is breaking—I shall tell you what I would have you do. Good-night. Remember you have given me your promise."

"I swear to you, mother," said Seraph, overcome by sudden emotion and dropping on his knees before her, "I swear to do whatever you may command."

His mother smiled and, bending over him, imprinted a kiss upon his forehead.

Two days afterward Seraph was on his journey toward the south.

The journey was a tiresome one, through a country void of charm. The train rattled past wide, desolate plains, by the side of freshly ploughed fields, through straggling, mean villages. Rarely did a hill or even a church-spire break the monotony of the level landscape. When the border between Poland and Little Russia was crossed, the landscape grew every moment livelier and more cheerful. Now and then the train stopped at a town. The platform of the station was invariably crowded with Jews, who, clothed in their long black caftans, ran hither and thither like a swarm of busy ants. Sometimes a squad of Austrian soldiers marched past. Besides them, only the peasants clad in dirty blouses, ploughing with half-starved horses in the fields, and followed by flocks of crows, were to be seen. In vain did Seraph court sleep upon the way. Peace, happiness, had fled, and, as it seemed to him, forever. Gloomy forebodings tormented him, sad thoughts trooped through his mind.

In the early dawn the train stopped at a little out-of-the-way station, the end of his journey. He hired a small carriage to carry him westward over the mountains into Hungary. The sun was mounting higher and higher. The forests of the Carpathians were reddened by his rays. Long flights of birds flew past. Soon the aspect of the landscape changed entirely. The road wound upward through the forest. Through the green twilight of the arching trees, through which stray golden sunbeams sifted, came a balmy, spicy perfume. Finches and blackbirds were singing constantly. The red roofs of a village below glittered in the sun; the gilt cupola of a Greek church was turned to burnished, molten gold by its rays. Half-unconsciously Seraph's perturbed spirit was calmed and softened by the glad beauty of all around him. At an inn kept by a Jew they made a long halt. Very grateful it was too for the miserable, half-starved horses which drew the vehicle. After an hour's rest they resumed their journey. The road now led down a steep ravine. The carriage was roughly jolted over the stones and rocks lying in their way. At the bottom of the ravine a mountain torrent foamed. From here the road wound upward again and into a thick forest, which for a time completely shut out all view of the country around them. After an hour's drive the forest opened suddenly, and to the left a meadow covered with many-hued wild flowers appeared. The breeze blowing softly across the meadow wafted an intoxicating perfume. In the middle of this flowery plain they perceived a tall, spare man in the dress of a peasant, a hunting-pouch slung across one shoulder, a gun on the other. He was feeding two fawns with bread, which he held out to them in the palm of one hand. The noise of wheels passing caused the fawns to raise their shy brown eyes and gaze curiously at the carriage. The man too gazed at Seraph with eyes almost as full of wonder and as gentle as the fawns. He raised his hat, however, politely in response to Seraph's greeting.

"The man acts as if he had never seen a civilized being in his life before," remarked the Jew driver contemptuously to Seraph.

The trees now grew sparser and sparser; through the gaps between their trunks glimpses of fields and meadows appeared. They drove past a great, wide, desolate plain presently; a flock of sheep was browsing on it, watched by a great black wolf-hound. The shepherd lay face downward underneath an elder-bush, sound asleep. At the sight of the carriage the dog broke out into loud and furious barking. The noise woke the shepherd, who, seeing a traveller, sprang quickly to his feet and bowed smilingly.

He was a tall, slender young gypsy, bare-footed, and wearing a blouse of dirty linen. An embroidered cap was set jauntily on the top of the crisp, short curls of his black hair.

His smile revealed a long row of dazzlingly white teeth in strong contrast to his nut-brown face.

He picked up a violin from where it lay on the ground and went in pursuit of his flock with long, light gliding steps.   In the middle of the plain he halted suddenly and began playing on his instrument a wild, sweet, yearning melody.

At the sound of the music the lambs, as though in obedience to a call, came trooping round him on every side.

"Queer people," muttered the Jew from under his greasy black mustache, "very queer people, the gypsies.   Who ever heard before of a man playing the fiddle to a flock of sheep?"

Evening came on now.   The shadows had grown long, the sun was sinking.   Their road now lay along the river's bank.   Suddenly a sound of some one singing fell upon the ear.   It was a gay, fresh voice that sang a song cheerful as the bright blue sky, and yet as mysterious, as strange as the whis-perings of the rushes and willows that dipped their leaves and branches in the stream.   There was a clump of willows growing thickly at this spot.   Without waiting for Seraph's orders, the Jew stopped the horse and pointed with the handle of his whip through the trees. On a low overhanging branch of one of these willows a girl had made herself a seat. She was swaying idly backward and forward, dipping her small naked feet in the water and singing as she swayed. The face, neck, and arms were covered by a skin of a pale olive color; a flood of blue-black hair hung loose upon her shoulders. She turned a pair of large, dreamy black eyes curiously on Seraph. He in his turn could not take his admiring eyes from her charming face. There was a wild, untutored, almost gypsy-like grace about her every movement. A moment she sat there gazing, the next she had dipped one hand in the water and sent the drops plashing up into Seraph's face, then laughing gayly she disappeared.

The castle of Honoriec, standing on the top of a steep, precipitous rock, now loomed in sight. The descending twilight softened the outline of gray rock and brown tree-trunk and mossy, crumbling, ivy-hung walls. A great round tower leaned dark against the yellow sky. In the distant background the dark chain of the Carpathians was visible, the peaks still crimson from the after-glow. A strange, mysterious music filled the air about them. It was like the sound of the wind when it roars in the high tops of the pine trees, making them wail and sob. But there was no wind on this still evening, and yet the mysterious melody rose and fell around about them; it was as though a cloud of lost souls weeping, wailing for the Paradise forever shut to them were flying through the air. As the carriage drove up to the castle, the gates were opened for them as though by an invisible hand.

Seraph descended from it, and handing his card (one on which a false name was written) to a servant who came forward, he inquired if Pan Theodorowitsch was at home.

"Certainly," returned the servant, an old man, speaking in the confidential tone of a trusted domestic, "he is always at home at this hour."

"Say to him that I have arrived from Lemberg," added Seraph.

While the servant was gone on his errand, Seraph had time to look about him. Before him and directly opposite the great gates stood the main building.

The castle, a massive stone structure of Charles XII.'s time, bore upon its façade the carved escutcheon of the family. A flight of broad granite steps led up to the great entrance doors of oak, black with age.

Above the portal sprang a balcony of hewn stone resting on the shoulders of two turbaned and fettered Turkish figures.

In the left wing the blinds were drawn tightly down. The apartments there were evidently not in use. To the right of the main building was a round tower.

In front of this tower was a garden, which had been left to run wild. It had spread itself over the side of the declivity on which the tower was built. The painted windows of a small Gothic chapel to the left of the tower were glowing in the rays of the setting sun.

A great wolf-hound was lying before the
entrance door. He remained motionless,
gazing haughtily at the new-comer, his great
head resting on his huge paws.

Solitude reigned here, it was plain to be
seen, solitude but not desolation. Everything around the place wore the appearance
of order and comfort.

The servant returned presently, bidding
Seraph follow him. The visitor's heart beat
high as he entered the house. The servant,
preceding him, led the way through a great
drawing-room; Seraph followed him as
though he were walking in his sleep. They
went through a long suit of rooms, entering at last a small bow-windowed apartment, a study evidently. There the master of the house came forward to greet his
guest. He was a tall man with a stately
carriage. He had the face of a knight and
the eyes of a seer. He looked kindly yet
searchingly at Seraph. And this man was
a monster—a human vampire! Impossible,
Seraph told himself. This was his first
thought, but a second followed close upon

it. He recalled his mother's words, her warnings. He remembered his promise.

"You are welcome, Pan Stefanski," said Emilian, holding out his hand.

"Pardon me," said the young man, refusing the offered hand, "it is a mistake. I have inadvertently given the servant a card not my own. My name is not Stefanski. It is," he continued, looking straight into his host's eyes, "it is Seraph Temkin."

Emilian smiled. "Your name is of no consequence. One sees at the first glance that you are a gentleman."

"I am the son of Madame Temkin," Seraph repeated, wondering at the composure of his interlocutor, "a lady with whom you were once well acquainted." He paused, expecting Emilian to change color, to cringe, to tremble before him.

The latter smiled absently. "I have not the honor of knowing your mother, but I am charmed to make the acquaintance of her son. I never, to my knowledge, heard the name of Temkin before. But that does not matter." He offered his hand again to the young man, who accepted it hesitatingly.

"Oh," he murmured half under his breath, "I do not deserve such a welcome, so kind, so hospitable a welcome. I am quite a stranger to you."

Emilian motioned him to seat himself on a Turkish divan near by, and took the place beside him.

"Why so many words?" he said, smiling. "You have something very winning in your face, Pan Temkin. Your eyes—where have I seen eyes like yours before, I wonder?"

"My eyes are like my mother's, I have been told."

"Perhaps, and yet I have never, as I said before, never met your mother. Then too —it is strange—but your eyes, your clear, true, kind eyes, remind me strangely of some one I knew years ago—of one who was not kind, but cruel, pitiless. But there, the memory is not a pleasant one; we will put it aside from this moment on."

"You have never, then, met—never seen my mother, Madame Temkin?"

"As I told you before, the name is quite strange to me."

Seraph was silenced, puzzled. Could it be possible his mother had unwittingly sent him to the wrong person? He must wait— the future must decide what he must do. The curtain at the door rustled suddenly, and the brown nymph of the river-bank appeared between its folds. Seraph arose in astonishment; their eyes met. In her eyes surprise shone. His, however, rested on her almost sadly.

"Pan Seraph Temkin," said Emilian to her, "our guest, and not for a short time, I trust. And this is my little Magdalina—the elf—the fairy—the gypsy—what shall I call her?—of our household."

Magdalina shrugged her shoulders with a gesture half pettish, half childish, and began bashfully to strip the leaves off a willow wand she held in one hand. She had on a pair of red morocco boots with high silver heels which tinkled as she walked, a short petticoat of bright-colored stuff, a blue bodice, beneath which a full white embroidered shirt was visible; around her slender brown throat was clasped a collar of coral and gold, and on her dusky arms hung innumerable bangles of gold coins. A wreath of wild flowers was on her crisp dark hair. Her costume suited her strange wild beauty admirably. Seraph silently likened her to a bird of Paradise, gone astray in this Northern clime. Everything about her betrayed her Southern origin. Her slender, lithe, and supple figure, her dark cheeks on which burnt the vivid color of the pomegranate blossom, her dark flowing hair, her glowing, deep dark eyes.

"And now what has brought you here?" asked Emilian, looking affectionately at her.

"I came to tell you that dinner is on the table."

She nodded gayly and flew away like some great bright-hued butterfly.

Seraph looked after her enchanted. His real errand to the castle—the dark, hidden purpose which had sent him here—was quite forgotten.

CHAPTER II.

THERE were no other guests besides Seraph at dinner. Emilian exerted himself to the utmost to entertain the new-comer. While he spoke the young people exchanged shy, furtive glances across the dinner-table, although no word of his host fell unheeded on Seraph's ears. The favorable impression made from the first on him by Emilian grew and strengthened with every moment spent in his society. The master of the house in his turn regarded his unexpected guest with glances at once kind and searching. It appeared to him as if in some way this young stranger must at some period of his life have been closely and dearly connected with him. Yet that, he told himself, was impossible. The young man's face, his name, were quite strange to him.

When the dinner was over and they had lighted their cigars in the little drawing-room, Emilian inquired of his guest what had brought him to this lonely and out-of-the-world corner of Hungary.

It was a question difficult enough for him to answer. Magdalina came unconsciously to the rescue.

" You intend to make a tour in the mountains?"

"I had thought of doing so."

"Remain with us," exclaimed Emilian: "we can visit them together."

"You are too kind, Pan Theodorowitsch."

"Not at all. Come, I have a proposal to make you. Let Honoriec be your headquarters. From here you can explore the mountains with me, or alone, as it may suit your fancy. You can hunt, ride, fish, in the interval. There is no lack of amusement here for a young man fond of outdoor sports."

"I am greatly obliged to you."

"You accept the invitation, then?"

Seraph glanced at Magdalina, who was looking at him anxiously, as though fearing a refusal; he bowed assent.

Pan Theodorewitsch now rang for a servant, and gave orders for a chamber to be made ready for the guest. When the man returned with the information that all was in readiness, Theodorowitsch arose and turning toward Seraph said: "You are doubtless fatigued from your long journey. Allow me to accompany you to your room. I need not wish you 'good repose,' for at your age one sleeps well wherever one may happen to find one's self—in the open air, by the shepherd's fire, as well as on a bed of down."

Seraph was about to bid Magdalina "goodnight." He discovered, however, that she had vanished. At the door of his chamber Luka stood waiting, holding a candlestick high in one hand. "It is odd," said his host, when they were alone in the chamber together, "that you should have fancied that I had once known your mother. But I have been diligently rummaging every hole and cranny of my memory, without finding any name at all resembling that of Temkin. I have always prided myself on never forgetting either a name or a face. Once

again let me welcome you to Honoriec; I
hope you will long continue to be a guest
within its walls," he added, holding out his
hand to Seraph; then bidding him "good-
night" he quitted the apartment.

Seraph, left alone, fell a prey to uneasy
and reproachful thought. What would be
the end of his adventure? he mused.
Would it not be better to leave the place
at once—to flee by night—to return to his
mother and demand fuller, more complete
instructions concerning this task she had
given him? How could he go away now,
when he had seen her, this charming creature, half-child, half-woman, the angel of the
household? But to remain—to return hos-
pitality by treachery, cruel treachery, that
too was quite impossible. He walked restlessly up and down the apartment, finally
approached the window, and throwing it wide
open, looked out into the still, fragrant
darkness. A soft, strange, wild music filled
the air around about him. Seraph recognized the strains: it was the gypsy-shepherd
playing upon his violin in the meadow just

below. Suddenly a silver clear voice sang out an accompaniment to the music. It was Magdalina's voice. She sat perched upon the castle wall. The song, so cheerful, so bright, brought back hope and courage to the listener's sad heart. As Magdalina's voice died away, a low, mysterious, thrilling, almost unearthly music wailed high up above her head; the same music Seraph had heard as he entered the castle. This time, however, he recognized whence it came. An æolian harp was placed in one of the highest windows in the round tower; the soft spring wind blowing across its strings caused it to fill the air with wild, soft, mysterious music.

Days passed by, and this old castle of Honoriec, with its dim, mysterious corridors, its rooms filled with faded furniture and hung with moth-eaten tapestry, grew dearer and dearer to Seraph. He saw his host and Magdalina only at dinner. All day long he was at liberty to go and come as he pleased, to seek and find his own amusements. Each morning the lord of the castle rode off, followed by his ancient groom Gedeon and the gamekeeper Isar, on a tour of inspection of the estate. The great wolf-hound trotted off by the side of his master's horse, and Magdalina was always there to wave him an adieu as he rode away. When Emilian was away, Magdalina, in her turn, vanished from Seraph's sight. This departure of Emilian was the only incident, full of life and movement, of the day. Stillness brooded over the whole house, not a sad melancholy, but rather the calm of contentment and perfect peace. This peace, this calm, was of immeasurable benefit to Seraph's tossed and anxious soul. He quite forgot why he had come to this spot; it was as though a spell had been cast over him—a kindly spell, causing him to forget all cruelty, all wickedness, all injustice existing in the world outside of this enchanted place. He sat long hours in the garden, a book in his hand which he forgot to open. On the bench beneath the shade of a great lime-bush, where the sun could only peep, now and then, through a small rift in the thickly leaved

branches, he sat listening to the songs of the
finches and linnets, the thrushes and robins,
that nested among the leaves. Now and
then a small brown lizard glided or a little
green serpent wriggled among the fallen
leaves at his feet; or high above, in the blue
air, he would see an eagle sailing majesti-
cally, poised on wide-spread wings. Sometimes the branches of the tree would be put
aside with a quick, light touch, and Magdalina's olive face and great dark eyes would
shine out at him from among the veiling
leaves; the next moment the branches had
fallen back again—she was gone as quickly
as she had come. Only when Emilian and
Seraph were drinking tea after dinner in the
little drawing-room did the girl begin her
pretty pranks—wandering, like some bright-
winged butterfly, restlessly from one corner
of the room to the other, now half-buried in
some great old leather-covered chair, now
perched uneasily on a high carved music-
stool, singing half under her breath little
scraps of song; sometimes disappearing
altogether for a while, to return clanking in

a suit of winged armor of some ancestor of Emilian's of King Sobieski's time, or waving above her curly head a tattered and faded Turkish banner, a world too heavy for the tiny hands that struggled to hold it aloft. When Seraph had retired to his chamber, the strange charm of this existence, so romantic, so solitary, and so sweet, became imbued with added charms. The tall old trees outside the casement rustled and whispered to one another mysteriously; the soft melody of the æolian harp filled the air in accompaniment to Magdalina's voice singing some old Hungarian slumbersong in the room above his own. The voice, the slender, girlish figure with its bright innocent eyes, haunted his dreams.

So passed day after day. Seraph had quite forgotten the outside world—a world full of toil and care, of sorrow and revenge —in the Arcadian life about him. The errand which had brought him to Honoriec was quite forgotten.

The Sunday after his arrival at the castle he had ridden off to church in the neighboring village. Magdalina had waved him adieu from her place on the tower, throwing down on his head a great shower of pine-cones as he rode off. Her song followed him as he went, rivalling that of the innumerable larks singing high in the sky above him.

The bells were ringing for service when Seraph arrived at the village of Wislonka. He drew rein and dismounted, tied his horse to the hedge, and watched the peasants, who, with their wives and children, were assembled around the open church-door. It was the first time he had ever seen the peasants of the Carpathian mountain region attired in their Sunday costume. He noticed that that of the men had something warlike and martial about it. They were clad in tight, short breeches of leather and high laced boots; with broad leather girdles, mounted and clasped with silver, in which their long, sharp knives and short hatchets were stuck. Over their full, loose white shirts a short jacket of cloth or velvet was worn. From one shoulder hung the sardak

4

(dolman). The jacket and sardak were always of some bright color—red, blue, white, or vivid green. The broad-brimmed hats of felt were decked with peacock's feathers or hung around with coins and medals of gold or silver. The women wore short, bright-colored petticoats; like the men, they too wore the sardak hanging from one shoulder. It was heavily trimmed with coral ornaments or gold coins. They also carried the "*torpor*" (hatchet) in their broad leathern belt. Men and women all had tall, slender, upright figures, sunburned brown faces, and great flashing dark eyes.

As he stood there, somebody suddenly grasped his arm and a voice cried: "Fellow-student, what in the name of Heaven brings you to this wilderness?"

Turning, Seraph looked down into the astonished eyes of his friend, Marzin Zepharowitsch.

"This is then your native village?"

"Yes: my father has charge of the orthodox Greek church here."

"How could I have forgotten that?"

"You have probably had more important things to think about; but service is beginning—let us go into the church."

They entered and stood a moment beneath the organ-loft, looking around them. In one of the pews reserved for the clergyman's family and strangers, Seraph noticed the charming face of a young girl. Her great childish eyes were now lowered devoutly on her prayer-book, now raised piously toward the vaulted ceiling, while the red, full lips murmured prayers unceasingly. A long, light-brown braid of hair, which had become loosened and fallen on one plump shoulder, was tossed contemptuously in its place again.

"Who is that pretty girl in the pew yonder," whispered Seraph to his companion, "the one sitting next the fat lady in the horrid blood-red gown?"

"As the girl is my sister I cannot really be a judge if she is pretty or not, and the lady in the horrid blood-red gown is her and my mother."

"Are you aware that you never even told me that you had a sister?"

"Indeed, I never imagined the information would be of interest to you."

"She is charming—an angel of beauty!"

"A very chubby-cheeked angel, I am afraid."

"Do not blaspheme, I implore you."

"I am dumb."

When the service was over Zepharowitsch insisted on Seraph's going home with him without waiting for an introduction to the family. He took his guest up into his own chamber, filled a pipe for him and a small glass of kontuschuwla (a strong brandy made from corn). When they had finished their pipes and glasses, Zepharowitsch proposed to his friend to go into the sitting-room. It was furnished with old-fashioned oak furniture, the chairs and couch covered with brilliant-flowered woollen stuff. From the middle of the ceiling hung a large chandelier of gilded wood; against one side of the wall leaned an old harpsichord, probably dating from the time of Mozart.

"Who is there?" asked a voice from an adjoining chamber.

"I, mother, with my friend Pan Temkin."

"Oh, I will be with you directly." And following the words, a majestic personage sailed in—a personage whose appearance probably excited feelings of admiring awe in the bosoms of the peasants and choir-boys of her husband's congregation.

Madame Zepharowitsch had donned a cap with vivid green ribbons in honor of her son's guest.

"What an honor!" she exclaimed. Then added the usual form of greeting in Hungary, "The blessing of God be upon you."

"I fall at your feet, madame."

"You will honor our poor roof by remaining under it?"

"You are too good, but I am at present the guest of Pan Emilian."

"With Emilian Theodorowitsch?" returned the lady, vainly trying to conceal her astonishment. "But that is something quite unusual. Honoriec is like a king's palace, I have been told."

Her husband now came into the room and greeted Seraph kindly. He had a tall, lean, gaunt figure, surmounted by a kindly, sensible face. His daughter came tripping smilingly after him. "My sister Milena," said Zepharowitsch, "my friend Pan Temkin," introducing them to each other. "I have often spoken to you of him," he continued, addressing his sister.

"Yes, indeed," returning Milena, casting a shy glance in Seraph's direction; "he drew a rather awful picture of you too. You were, according to him, a young man who neither danced, nor sung, nor conversed—one whose sole diversion was practising shooting at a mark with a pistol."

"I do not understand," returned Seraph, "how your brother, whom I thought a friend, could have drawn such an unflattering picture of me. But though I might find it possible to forgive that, I cannot forgive his never having spoken of his charming sister to me."

"He had probably more important subjects to speak about."

"Impossible, mademoiselle. What more agreeable subject could he have found to speak about? I can assure you I shall find it hard to pardon your brother's forgetfulness."

"We trust," interrupted her mother here, "we shall often have the pleasure of seeing Pan Temkin in our humble home."

Already in her mind's eye she saw her daughter's head crowned with the betrothalwreath.

"I cannot suppose," interposed her husband, "that Pan Temkin would care to often leave the society of such a man as Theodorowitsch to seek ours."

"You are a friend of his, then?" asked Seraph eagerly. "You are well acquainted with him?"

"Do I know him?" was the answer. "No one knows him better than I or honors him more. How many nights we have passed together studying the stars! Emilian is the best, the noblest man in the world. At once great and magnanimous, yet simple. He is everything a man should be—nothing is wanting."

"But I have heard——"

"It does not matter what you have heard. Whoever spoke a word against your host lied—lied wilfully, basely. He was unhappily married. His wife was—but—well, we will not speak of her. Young man, I have lived long and know the world well; there are women who, for a caprice, will throw a pearl of great price down a deep well and quarrel with a man for not fetching it up again for them."

On his way home Seraph fell in with the gamekeeper. "Why do you carry your gun along with you on Sunday?" he asked the man, handing him a cigar as he spoke.

"I came here to look after my lord's deer. He did not give me any orders to do so, but for a master like him one does what one can unbidden."

Seraph rode on, more and more puzzled. Could it be this man, whose goodness formed a theme for every tongue, who had rendered his mother's life miserable? Impossible!

The very next morning, shortly after breakfast, Seraph stumbled accidentally into the baking-room. The door stood open, and the cook, with her sleeves rolled up, was kneading vigorously a great batch of dough.

A bright-colored little figure sat on the broad window-seat, watching the process of bread-making—a figure which at sight of Seraph fluttered quickly away. He hastened after this flying figure through the court-yard, garden, and into the chapel, where it had fled for refuge, but never a trace of Magdalina, for it was she, could he find.

He flew up the stairs which led to the organ-loft. Hardly was he there, when a clear, mocking laugh from below was heard, and a red skirt fluttered out of the door, through the court-yard, and into the castle again.

Renewed flight and pursuit now followed. Through the large drawing-room they sped into the smaller one, then along the wide corridor, up the great staircase, until the attic was reached. Here by a dormer-window leading out on the leads Seraph made sure of his game. But in the twinkling of an eye the daring girl was out upon the

sloping roof, from where she slid quickly
down into the gutter running along the
edge, and springing on the great dragon
which served as a spout to carry off the
rain, swung herself down, by means of an
overhanging branch of a tree which grew
below, into the court-yard beneath, while
Seraph, amazed and almost doubting his
eyes, made his way after her, rather shame-
facedly, by means of the staircase. When
he descended thither he saw something scarlet, like a great red poppy, glimmering
among the foliage of the vines that covered
the high brick wall. He grasped hastily at
the object, but it eluded his grasp, and
Magdalina's mocking laughter echoed from
the other side of the wall. To scale it was
for him only the work of a moment, but on
looking about him he could see no trace of
her. Just then he heard his name called
from above, and looking upward he saw
Magdalina's bright eyes flashing down at
him from among the leaves of a great lime-
tree, on one of whose branches she had
perched herself. He began at once to climb

up after her, and as he swung himself out
on the branch where Magdalina was sitting
he exclaimed, "I have caught you at last,
mademoiselle."

"Yes, you have caught me, because I was
too tired to go on, else I could have swung
myself down on the other side while you
were climbing up." She leaned back against
the cradling bough; her white teeth were
gleaming through her red parted lips, her
cheeks fairly blazing with color, her dark eyes
flashing with mirth. She seemed to Seraph
at this moment like no earthly maiden; she
was rather a great bright flower swaying
there among the green shimmering leaves.

"Do you really think you could have
caught me if I had not let you?" she asked.
"How charming it is here," she went on
dreamily; "one can see everything without
being seen in return. I should like to be so
high up that I could look down and see the
whole wide world lying below me at a
glance."

"That would be impossible, I fear, for you
know the earth is round——"

"As if I did not know that," she returned scornfully. "Oh, I know a great deal more than you think I do—Emilian has taught me. One would be stupid, indeed, not to be able to learn from a master like him. But from a star one could at least see a good deal below, I am sure. I remember, as though it were in a dream, a beautiful woman who, when I was a little, little child, used to hold me in her lap and tell me many pretty tales. She told me once the stars were golden chairs in which the saints sat."

"You say Emilian has taught and cherished you, mademoiselle, and yet you do not call him 'father.'"

"Why should I call him father? He is not my father."

"Pardon me if I have been impertinent."

"I do not know what it is you mean. Nobody has ever asked me a question like that before. I do not know how or when it was I came here; I only know I have not always lived here or with Emilian. Where I lived first there were many, many people; it was a large house, and the beautiful wo-

man who kissed me and told me tales used
to go riding with many other ladies and
gentlemen. I remember, too, the horse she
rode. It was a white one, and the lady—my
lady I mean—used to wear a black habit, a
high hat like a man's, and carry a gold-
·handled whip; but it is all dim and faint, as
though I had dreamed it long ago.

"But Emilian—he is an angel of goodness
and kindness. I owe him everything. I
could not love him more were he really my
father. He is my father, benefactor, master, all in one. I do not know, I cannot
remember when it was that he brought me
here. I only know that I love and honor
him above every other being in the whole
wide world."

Seraph listened to her in silence, pro-
foundly touched by her innocent expressions
of love and gratitude toward her benefactor.
And so they sat, these two young creatures,
aloft in the great branches of the lime-
tree, like two birds who have sought and
found a place to build their nest.

CHAPTER III.

O N that same evening after dinner, Emilian proposed to them to go up on the tower and look at the stars in his company. On Seraph's consenting, he rang the bell for Luka, whom he ordered to fetch a lantern and accompany them. The old man went off, returning presently with a long, wide mantle with hanging sleeves, which he hung on his master's shoulders, then handed him a round close cap, which made him look a veritable astrologer. "Shall I fetch a mantle for the young gentleman?" Luka inquired. Seraph declined the mantle, and Luka lighting the wax taper in the lantern he had fetched, they passed out of the door on the way to the round tower.

"Where is Magdalina?" asked Emilian as they were walking through the courtyard.

"Here I am," she answered, suddenly ap-

pearing out of darkness and thrusting her
arm through his.

"How odd you look!" he exclaimed, looking down at her.

"Like a bat, do I not?" she returned merrily. She had wrapped around her a wide
mantle of black and gray silk; a small black-
lace veil was wrapped entirely around her
head, its two long pointed ends thrown back
like wings on each side of her face.

"Like a great bat indeed," said Seraph.

"A vampire," returned Magdalina, turning her head in his direction, and stretching
out her hands with the fingers bent like
claws, she made a gesture as though she
would tear out his heart.

"I am not afraid of this vampire," said
Seraph, laughing.

"You are a man," she answered with
sudden gravity, "and should be afraid of
nothing."

They ascended the steep winding stair of
the tower. Luka set down the lantern upon
a ledge near by and withdrew noiselessly.
The wide star-bespangled sky above their

heads seemed to bend benignantly over them. Magdalina laid her hand softly on Seraph's shoulder as they stood there side by side.

"How beautiful it is up here," she began softly. "I am always happy when the earth lies so far below me. I think I feel as a bird must when he flies high, high up in the air, far above the very highest trees. Do you know the names of the stars? I know a few of them—only a few. There, straight above our heads, you can see Charles' wain. Does it not look as if it were made of great sparkling jewels? Yonder is Cassiopeia's chair. If you could bind the five stars together with lines, they would form a great W. Where are the Pleiades? I cannot find them." And Magdalina let her eyes wander searchingly over the sky.

While she had been talking, Emilian had set up and arranged the great telescope. He now turned to Seraph, and addressing him said: "The study of astronomy, the perusal of the heavens, has been a great consolation, a resource, to me of late years. When one studies those great and mysterious worlds yonder, one forgets one's self and one's petty griefs and cares. One soars upward and onward, leaving this dull earth behind. After all, what is this world—this planet we live upon—but a point, a dot in the universe hardly larger than one of those glimmering dots of the Milky Way?" Emilian continued to speak and the young man listened reverently, his eyes fastened on the pale, thoughtful face of his host. How dear it had grown to him day by day, this countenance in which truth and goodness beamed.

Seraph could hardly realize that he had come to this man with hate in his heart, with thoughts of revenge filling his mind. Now the majesty of a true, good, and simple life, a life passed in works of love and kindness toward others, made him realize how poor, how wicked, how hollow his own had been. He would have liked to have fallen down at the feet of this man, to implore his pardon, to ask for his love, this man whom Seraph knew only too well was quite indifferent to his hate as to his love.

When they descended from the tower the

5

frosty breath of early dawn was stirring among the leaves. In the east, a long bright streak announced the coming of the sun. The planet Venus, on the edge of the horizon, shone through a misty veil of cloud. All was silent, expectant, awaiting the coming of the God of Day. ⌒

Seraph and his host bade each other "good-night" in the drawing-room. Magdalina's eyes, usually so bright, were blinking sleepily.

Summer had come in the night. The air was hot and still. The dust lay thick in the road and on the leaves of plants and trees. Everything living longed and thirsted for rain. The castle was quieter, more slumberous than ever. After an early dinner that day, Emilian proposed an excursion to the forest. Seraph and Magdalina each armed themselves with a gun; the old wolf-hound left his place before the castle-door to follow his master. The sun hung like a great fiery ball above the mountains.

They crossed a great meadow on their way. A hare sprang up from the grass at

their feet, ran a short distance, then squatted
down to look anxiously at the dog by Emilian's side. ' Looking down in the grass at
their feet, they saw a young hare lying
there trembling. Emilian called the dog to
him, and on looking backward, after going
a few feet, they saw the mother hurrying
back to her young one. The cheerful whistle
of a quail was heard at intervals.

They now entered the forest.

A path wound itself before them; the in-
terlocked branches of the tall pine trees
formed a green arched roof above. The
ground, strewn with pine-needles and moss,
was like a velvet carpet to their tread.

A doe followed by two fawns sprang
across their path. "How tame the creatures
seem hereabouts," Seraph observed to Magdalina, who was walking by his side.

"It is owing to Emilian," she returned;
"he will not have them hunted or killed."

The path growing narrower led now down
a ravine. Complete silence reigned here; no
bird sang, not even a twig rustled. It was
like the majestic, solemn stillness of a tem-

ple not made with hands. Now and then
a pine-cone dropped from the trees above
noiselessly to the ground. This silence was
suddenly broken by the baying of a dog,
followed by the report of a gun.

The gamekeeper Igar came toward them.
"God save you," he called out.

"What are you doing here, Igar?" inquired his master. "Why did you fire your
gun off just now?"

"I fired at a great vulture which only
yesterday killed one of our young fawns.
Unfortunately I missed him. The creature
is more cunning than I."

"Why are you watching for him here?"
inquired Magdalina.

"Do you see the dead fir-tree yonder,
mademoiselle, the one split asunder from a
hurricane? There on the highest bough the
robber perches in the evening after he has
gorged himself. That is his perch, and I
have just scared him away from it; but he
will be back again presently, I know. He
has eaten too much to be able to fly far."

Magdalina drew a long breath, and taking the gun off her shoulder examined it closely.

They continued on their way. Emilian had taken Seraph's arm and was speaking to Igar, who walked a few steps behind them. They had gone some distance before they became aware that Magdalina was not with them.

"Let me go back for her," proposed Seraph.

"No, no; you would probably not find her, and lose your way besides."

"Let us call to her." Igar placed a hand on each side of his mouth and shouted loudly: "Mademoiselle! mademoiselle!" Only echo answered him mockingly. Again he shouted; no reply. Then all three lifted their voices in concert and called, "Mademoiselle! Magdalina! mademoiselle!" The echo returned the cries from all sides, like a chorus of teasing gnomes.

"If anything should have happened to her," murmured Emilian, much distressed.

"We must turn back and seek her," said Seraph resolutely.

They retraced their steps, but they had not gone a long way when a gun was fired off once, then a second time.

"What can that mean?" exclaimed Seraph, greatly alarmed. "Two shots. Can it be possible any harm has come to her?"

"There was only one shot," replied Igar; "the other was the echo of the first one." The dog now set off, running in the direction from which the sound of the shot had come. "Do not be alarmed," Igar continued reassuringly; "one does not shoot young ladies in this country. It will be mademoiselle who has shot, and she has hit the mark or she would have fired again."

The glad barking of the dog was now heard, and Magdalina appeared from among the surrounding trees, running to meet them. She carried her gun in one hand and a great vulture in the other. "There is the robber, the murderer!" she exclaimed exultingly to Emilian, "which killed your fawn," throwing the bird down at his feet.

"Brava!" he exclaimed, "a capital shot."

Seraph looked at her half-admiringly, half-disapprovingly. Her cheeks were glowing, her eyes sparkling gleefully.

"Why do you examine me so?" she asked of him.

"Could you have killed a dove with the same joy as you did this creature?" he inquired, looking straight into her eyes.

"Kill a dove? How could you think of such a thing?" she returned reproachfully. "Do I look so cruel, so bloodthirsty? But to shoot a robber—a murderer who has just killed one of my poor, pretty little fawns? Is it possible you object to that? There are a great many shy, innocent, gentle creatures that live in this forest. Should one not protect them, or rather leave them to be slaughtered ruthlessly?"

"No, no," returned Seraph quickly. "You are right. Forgive me for misjudging you, even for a second."

The gamekeeper slung the vulture across his shoulders, and they continued on their way, Seraph and Magdalina dropping a little behind.

"Do you think," the poor child resumed, evidently deeply wounded that Seraph, even for a moment, should have thought her cruel, "that Emilian would have praised me if I had not done right to shoot the vulture? He will only allow the noxious animals who inhabit this forest to be destroyed; and he is lord of the soil—of all the land about here as far as the eye can reach. No deer, or hare, or pheasant is ever killed on his domain. And that is the reason that the creatures are all as tame, as confiding about here as they were once in Paradise."

"Emilian certainly appears to be a man with a kind and gentle heart. Do you think it possible, could you ever believe that he could once have been cruel, pitiless, and that toward a woman—a woman who loved him?"

"Never! He could not be. It is impossible."

The forest had now gradually grown less dense; a great meadow covered with wild flowers lay before them. The sun was sinking in a background of golden and crimson clouds. A thrush, sitting upon a low-hanging branch of a larch-tree, burst into sudden song. A little brook rippled past them, a crowd of butterflies and bright-colored moths floating above its crystal clear waters. Emilian threw himself down beside it. Igar, with the dog at his feet, lay down a little distance off. Magdalina, stooping down, began plucking the flowers that grew in profusion about them. When she had filled the skirt of her frock with bright-colored blossoms, she came back, and seating herself on a stone, near which Seraph was lying, she began to weave a wreath of the flowers she had gathered. Placing this wreath on her hair, she got up and began slowly dancing backward and forward. It was the slow, graceful, un-dulating dance of some Eastern clime, a dance that might have been learned behind the curtains of an Eastern seraglio. Seraph could hardly take his eyes away from her. The graceful, sinuous movements of her lissome figure were accompanied by bend-ings of her long throat and glances of inno-cent coquetry from her dark, childish eyes.

The sun had set when Emilian gave the signal for their return. On reaching the road, they saw a cavalcade of riders coming toward them—a lady, young, slight, fair-haired, in the centre of a group of cavaliers. Her long habit floated in the breeze, a little square Polish cap surmounted her blond braids. She rode like a queen in the midst of her courtiers. The lady cast a look of surprise at Seraph and bowed gayly as she rode by him. He returned the greeting with a surprise no less than her own. It was Barbara, Madame Trendaloska. What has brought her here to this wilderness? was his thought as he looked back at her. She galloped quickly past him; a cloud of dust soon hid her and her train from sight.

The sun was gone, though the purple, gold, and crimson had not yet faded out of his attendant clouds. They formed a glowing background for the dark branches of the trees. The road ran along the banks of a stream, the gorgeous colors of the clouds reflected on its smooth, shining surface. The nightingales set up their song. The quiet beauty of the eventide had caused Seraph for a time to forget his companions in its contemplation, but he now became aware that Magdalina's mirth had departed. She had seated herself on a stone by the wayside; great tears were running down her cheeks.

"What is it, Magdalina?" he asked, alarmed. "What has happened? Why do you weep?"

"It is nothing, nothing at all," she returned pettishly, turning her head away.

"But you are crying."

"I—no," she forced herself to smile, and continued: "I must have run a thorn into my foot, I think."

Seraph knelt down, drew off the little shoe and silken stocking, and sought diligently for the offending thorn. In vain. The thorn she spoke of had not pierced her foot but her little jealous heart, which ached and ached since meeting with the beautiful lady riding past like a queen with her courtiers.

CHAPTER IV.

ON their return to Honoriec, after tea had been drunk in the drawing-room Seraph went out into the garden. It was a mild, bright night. The moon, large and red, sailed slowly away in the sky above, its rays filling court and garden with silvery light. The waters of the fountain sparkled, rainbow-colored. A sound of music came from within the chapel. Some one was playing on the organ there, playing with a master's hand.

Seraph pushed the door open and entered.

The chapel was filled with the soft radiance of the moonlight, which had filtered through the painted windows. The light fell upon the marble statues of the saints, their white faces seeming to smile. The image of the Mother of God seemed crowned with white, celestial roses; upon the dark floor of porphyry white pearls were strewn.

76

Seraph ascended the stairs leading up to the organ-loft. There he found Emilian seated before the organ, playing, his face deathly white in the ghostly light of the moon. He went on playing, not knowing that he was no longer alone. When at the end of his theme Seraph spoke, he turned with a start of astonishment.

"You here!" he exclaimed.

"Pardon the intrusion, but it was your playing that drew me here."

Emilian shook his head slightly, incredulously.

"You, young and happy—what charm can such music find for you? God forbid, too, that it should! Such music as mine is only for the lonely—the forsaken, the old."

"But I can understand it, I think; at-least I know and can appreciate its beauty, though as yet I have never known sorrow or despair. But forgive me the question—why should you have done with hope, with joy, with the world? Why pass your days in a solitude so obscure—you whose talents, whose character would command respect wherever they were known?"

"To answer you that," returned Emilian sadly, "would take a long time. It is really not possible to tell you all the reasons for my living the life I do; but I can tell you some which may, perhaps, be interesting and even valuable to you. After all, it is the duty of the old to give the young a leaf or two out of their experience, that the latter may avoid the thorns and escape, if possible, the pitfalls into which they themselves have fallen."

"Ah, how can I ever thank you for your kindness, your consideration for me?" murmured Seraph, a vague feeling of sadness oppressing him. A sensation of unreasoning and blind terror followed. Did he, perhaps, stand at the threshold of the secret chamber where his mother's sorrows and wrongs lay hidden?

Emilian struck a few lingering chords upon the organ-keys, then turning, he faced Seraph, who was standing behind him.

"It is a question," he said, more to himself

than to his listener, "whether it is after all better for us to be brought up far from the bustling world, and high above its sordid cares and selfish struggles, or rather to jostle with the crowd, pushing and being pushed by it. In the first instance, one enters the world, full of high thoughts and noble aspirations, but there is the danger of finding one's self misunderstood, perhaps even derided and cruelly deceived; then on the other hand, we are apt to fall into the error, an unamiable, an almost unpardonable one in youth, of distrusting and cruelly misjudging those who would have gladly been our friends if we would have permitted them to be so. We shut our door on happiness, only to realize that the bright guest has gone when it is too late. We distrust love, we welcome hate. We distrust our friends or turn them into foes—bitter, life-long foes.

"As for me, I was the only child of a widowed mother. I was brought up and educated far from the world. I had inherited the gentle disposition and kind heart of my mother. I could not knowingly have

trodden on a worm. ⁄ When I entered the
society of those of my own age, I was enchanted with everything I saw, with every
new friend I made.   I was incapable of distrust or suspicion.   The gay world in which
I lived seemed a veritable paradise to me—a
paradise where no serpent lurked.   Then I
first fell in love.   The object of my boyish
affection was a distant cousin, who had been
brought up in my mother's house as her own
child.   I found, on my return home from
the university to spend the summer holi-
days, that the child had grown to a woman
during my absence, a woman whose beauty
fairly dazzled me.   The fair hair was like
the sunshine to my eyes, her voice like the
voices of singing birds in the spring to my
ears.   I loved her from a distance, and
silently.   The great affection I bore her
made me appear shy and awkward in her
society.   How I ever found courage at last
to avow my love for her and receive her as-
surance that this love of mine was returned,
I do not know.   Suffice it to say, I loved
and was beloved in return.   But alas! my

idol was not all gold as I had imagined;
like many another, its feet were of clay.
Blessed by nature with so many gifts, with
a lovely face, and a disposition exceptional in
its gentleness, she was lacking in sincerity
and steadfastness. On my second visit to
my home from the university, I found, to
my great amazement, a change in her treatment of me. She appeared formal, ab-
sent, cold. This change in her behavior
lasted, however, for only a day or two after
my return; at the end of the week she was
again all tenderness and sweetness. Shortly
after, however, she confessed to me with
tears and sobs that a marriage had been
arranged for her by her guardians. She
promised, however, to be faithful to me, to
reject the obnoxious suitor, to wait until, my
course of study finished at the university, I
would be free to marry her. I returned to
town again, happy and secure, carrying with
me her promise of faithfulness. I had been
at the university hardly a month, when
cards of her betrothal were handed to me.
What I suffered at this time from the

6

wreck of my love and trust, I will spare you
the recital. Some years passed by before I
returned again to my home. When I did I
found my former *fiancée* a guest of my
mother's. The girl I had loved was transformed into an elegant woman of the world,
brilliant and coquettish. My heart beat
high when I first saw her, but I soon discovered that my love for her was dead—
killed by her own inconstancy. This, however, she refused to believe, to understand.
She confided to me her disappointment—
her grief. It was the old, old story. She
had married, but did not love her husband.
She had sold herself for fortune, for rank.
Now, however, she longed for affection—a
friend in whom she could confide her sorrows, her disillusions. The rôle she would
have given me I declined. Her siren song
fell on an ear deaf as Ulysses. This heartless
coquette, who had deceived me and would
deceive her husband, I despised. When at
last she perceived this, when it became ap-
parent to her that her blandishments fell on
a cold heart and deaf ears, her love turned

to hatred. She left my mother's house suddenly, and two years after she separated from her husband and vanished from our world. About the same time my mother died, and I was left alone. It was then that the thought of marriage presented itself again and again to my mind. I was not, I felt, made to live alone. The loss of my mother had left a great void in my life. My friends, too, urged me to marry. Many matches were suggested to me, but I had determined to choose a wife for myself. As you will see," Emilian interpolated here, sighing, "experience does not always give us wisdom. Deceived by a woman of gentle, charming manners, I fell into the opposite error of believing that only a cold and reserved woman could be a faithful one.

"Yet, after all, it was an accident that fixed my choice of a wife. Riding one day through a village, I heard a cry of 'Mad dog! mad dog!' raised suddenly, and a cur with foaming mouth and bent-down head ran blindly past me. Every one fled at the sight of him. Just then, however, the garden gate of a house beside the street was opened quickly. A young, slight girl stepped out and stood directly in the path of the infuriated brute.

"She held a pistol in one hand. Raising it and taking deliberate aim, she fired at the dog.

"He fell to the ground for an instant. The next he had staggered howling to his legs again, when the girl with a second shot stretched him lifeless to the ground. The creature rolled over dead in the dust of the road. At that moment, my young friend, I fell in love for the second time in my life, and the last. This girl, I learned, was the daughter of a retired army officer, a cavalry major, the owner of a small property in the neighborhood. Her mother was dead. The father busied himself with the care of the estate. His daughter, the eldest of the family, took charge of the house and her little brothers and sisters. The whole management of the household was in her hands.

"She drove to town to make purchases for the housekeeping, she rode with her father

to the fields to oversee the laborers, she
looked after the kitchen and the cow-stables.
The servants obeyed her implicitly, as did
her little brothers and sisters, whom she ruled
with an iron hand. Still, though severe, she
was not in the least cruel or unjust. It was
this severity of hers that gave her additional
charm in my eyes.

"When I told her of my love and asked
her to marry me, she gazed at me at first
with astonishment. It was evident the
thought of love, of marriage, had never
occurred to her. Then smiling proudly, she
placed her hand in mine. 'Forever?' I said
as I clasped the small yet strong hand in my
own. 'Forever,' she replied solemnly. And
I was then, for a short time, unspeakably
happy. Not for long, however. I soon perceived that she did not love me; she simply
permitted me to love her.

"When I sat near her and would have em-
braced her, she drew back smilingly and
said, 'That is all very well, but it is not
what I want; you must obey me.'

"'There are men,' I returned, 'who must

and will rule over a woman, while others
find it possible to obey her. It is not so
with me, however. I wish neither to be a
tyrant nor a slave. My wife will not stand
above or below me, but at my side. For
that reason I chose you. I know you are
strong, faithful as a man would be.'

"'Indeed I am strong,' she returned with
a mischievous look at me.

"'Strong enough to make me obey you?'
I asked her laughingly.

"'Certainly,' she returned quietly. She
seemed quite sure of her power to do so.

"Here I knew, however, that she deceived
herself. I am not the man to wear a yoke,
not even the flowery yoke of a beloved and
loving wife.

"The wedding took place at her father's
house with great pomp, ceremony, and feasting. While the guests were engaged in
dancing and feasting, I proposed to her that
we should take our departure quietly. She
looked at me with wide-open eyes of surprise.

"'Do you think I will go to my new home
under cover of night and darkness?' she

asked scornfully. ''I will have a grand welcome. The people must know and see they have a mistress. Send off a messenger at once to your steward, so that I may be received in a manner befitting me.'

" The next day my wife arrived at my castle as a queen enters her kingdom. She sat in a sledge drawn by eight horses, wrapped from head to foot in ermine, and nodded condescendingly to the peasants and servants who had come to greet her. The church bells rang a clashing, merry peal as we drove through the castle gates. Before the door stood the steward, bareheaded, to hand the customary offering of bread and salt, which is always offered by the servants and tasted by the new mistress before she sets foot across the threshold. She received this offering as a queen of old might have received the homage of a slave.

" Before our honeymoon was over, I knew my married life would never be what I had fondly fancied it. My wife never had an hour in the day to spend alone with me. From my wedding-day a sharp thorn pierced into my heart. She was my wife, and I loved her; but she had no love, it seemed, to waste on me or any one. I will not affirm that she had no heart, but it was incased in ice—no, not that either, for ice one can melt; her heart was rather imbedded in a case of stone, like those insects one often sees imbedded in amber. One must break, crush the stone if one would have the thing within it. It is impossible for me, however, to crush a woman's will either by cruelty or indifference. I could only bear my lot quietly, uncomplainingly. But I grew reserved, cold, toward my wife. She, however, never seemed to notice this change in me. A year after our marriage a son was born to us, and on this child I lavished all my affection. Then, to my great surprise, my wife began to exhibit signs of jealousy, dislike even, toward the babe she had borne. It was plain to be seen that she was unreasoningly, frantically jealous, not alone of the women we met, but even of the men for whose society I manifested a preference. She could hardly endure the visits of the village clergyman, who often came of an evening to play chess with me.

"What a strange temperament was hers! Incapable of love or tenderness, yet devoured by frantic and unreasonable jealousy. She grew every day more restless and unhappy. She flew into fits of ungovernable anger, and overwhelmed me with reproaches at my treatment of her. And yet, and yet—shall I confess it?—I was not at this time quite unhappy, nor did I regret that I had made her my wife. Life is, after all, a makeshift, and happiness never comes along the road we look for it.

"My wife's jealousy was, on the whole, rather flattering than otherwise, and nothing like as disagreeable to me as her indifference would have been. Then, too, our child—ah, what a delight, a never-ending source of happiness, pure and unalloyed, was this child to me! As I told you before, the mother was jealous, quite unfeignedly jealous, of the child, her own child, and it will not surprise you when I tell you that the nurse we had for him was the object of suspicion and aversion of my wife. This nurse was a beautiful peasant woman, from the province of Galicia. She was tall and well made, her face a perfect oval, lighted up by a pair of pensive blue eyes. She resembled one of Raphael's Madonnas. And this beautiful creature had, I must confess, a way of looking at me from out of those great dark-blue eyes which would have aroused the anger of a wife far less given to jealousy than mine was. When her services as nurse were no longer required, however, my wife, to my great surprise, retained her as an attendant to our child. What her motive was in doing so I have never been able to imagine. Days, months, years even went by, and we grew more and more estranged. At times my wife even exhibited signs of hatred and aversion toward me. She drove and rode out every day, but always alone. She paid visits and amused herself as it suited her, without consulting my tastes any way. She was seldom at home. This state of things grew worse. Often for months we hardly exchanged a word.

"One evening during the Carnival, my wife accompanied by a friend had gone to a ball in a distant town. I came back from hunting to find her away. I was very weary; we had killed more than a dozen wolves in the course of an afternoon. It was midnight when I returned. I changed my hunting suit for a dressing-gown and slippers, and went into the room where my little son was sleeping. To my surprise and vexation, I found the child alone, sleeping peacefully. I seated myself on the side of the bed, looking down on the sleeping little one, with a heart full of a joy that I would not have exchanged for any other in the world. Just then the nurse came into the room. 'Where is your mistress?' I inquired of her.

"'At a ball, gracious master,' was the answer.

"'And you,' I continued sternly, 'why did you leave the child alone in his room at this hour?'

"'I was only gone a moment,' she replied; then dropping her voice to a whisper she continued: 'Ah, do not look at me so sternly, gracious master. What man but you could look at a beautiful woman with such eyes as those?'

"I gazed at her in astonishment, but I was obliged to confess to myself as I looked that she was beautiful, perfectly beautiful, from the head, with its crown of brown plaits, to the tips of her small feet, shod in shoes of red leather with broad silver buckles.

"But I was not tempted by her beauty. I answered her in a voice which sounded cold and harsh even to my own ears: 'You are impertinent besides being neglectful of your duties. I shall see that my son has a more suitable person to watch over him.'

"She made no reply, only stood there with downcast eyes a moment; the next, she had thrown herself at my feet. She held me in an embrace from which it was impossible for me to free myself without violence; and— shall I, must I confess it?—rather than do this I submitted to her embraces, her caresses. My head reeled, my heart beat at the close contact of beauty so perfect—beauty that had thrown itself unsought into my arms.

Hardly knowing what I did, I stooped and kissed and kissed again and again the red, ripe lips held up to meet my own. A slight, muttered exclamation caused me to lift my head suddenly, and I beheld my wife standing there, a witness of all that had passed. She stood there one moment; the next, without a word or a second look in my direction, she turned and left the room. That very night in darkness and storm she fled from the house, carrying her child away with her.

"And from that day to this I have never set eyes on wife or child. I sought them over all Europe. For three long, weary years I sought them sorrowing—in vain. Two years after her flight I was told by a friend that he had seen my wife in Paris. I journeyed to Paris. I remained there six months. I employed the assistance of the police, I advertised in every newspaper, I spent a fortune in my search, but no trace of her could I find. At the end of three years I gave up all hopes, and retired to spend my life, my hopeless, joyless life, here."

Emilian left off speaking, burying his face in his hands.

Seraph too was silent, a prey of sad forebodings. Suddenly, however, he broke the silence: "Pardon, Pan Theodorowitsch, but since then did you never meet a woman whom you, had you been free, could have loved again?"

"Never—never; from that night I bade farewell to love—to hope, to happiness. I lived my life alone. And it is better so."

"And this woman—your wife—whom you sought so faithfully, whom you loved in spite of all, was she, could she have been perhaps—my mother?"

"Your mother?" returned Emilian, looking at him with cold surprise. "Your mother? What can have put such a thought into your mind? Did I not tell you from the very first moment of our meeting that I have never known any one of your name? What odd fancies romantic young people take into their heads," he added wearily.

CHAPTER V.

ERAPH was sitting in the garden the next day reading, when Luka came creeping up to him with his usual respectful bearing, trying, unsuccessfully, however, to conceal the knowing smile upon his shrivelled lips.

"A peasant woman, gracious master, is here who wishes to speak to you."

"A peasant woman?" returned Seraph indifferently. "Probably some one with a message from Pan Zepharowitsch. Where is she?"

Luka put aside the branches of an elder bush as though he were putting aside a portière, and called: "Here, come here! The gracious master will condescend to speak to you."

A young peasant woman of surpassing beauty appeared, and walking quickly up to Seraph, looked at him archly for a moment;

then, turning her back on him, buried her face in a lace handkerchief to stifle the laughter which shook her frame. Luka withdrew silently, all expression abstracted from his countenance. When he was gone the girl removed her handkerchief, and going up to Seraph, laid a little, white, bejewelled hand lightly on his shoulder. Seraph looked closely at the slight figure, the fresh, laughing face, the blue eyes brimming over with ill-suppressed mirth. "Barbara!" he exclaimed; then in a reproving tone: "What on earth possessed you to come here, and in that dress too?"

"It was in tones like yours that Orestes probably asked the Eumenides why they pursued him," she returned mockingly. "I came here because I wanted to see you."

"You think I am ass enough to believe that, Barbara?"

"You may believe, you must believe that I love you, Seraph."

"That you do not."

"You will acknowledge it one day, be sure of that," said Madame Trendaloska; "but I did not come here to quarrel with you, provoking as you are."

"Why have you come, I ask you for the second time?"

"I came to invite you to come to the house where I am visiting."

"You would like to add one more to the list of adorers."

"To-morrow a hunt will meet at Senbyn, the house of Countess Barvaroska; you must promise me to be one of it."

"I must?—pardon me, must is a word I do not understand."

"But you will come?"

"No."

"Idiot!" she exclaimed, stamping her little foot in a fury, and made a motion to leave him. Suddenly she turned and threw herself down on the seat beside him. Throwing her arms around him and putting her fresh, ripe lips close to his ear, she whispered, "Come, Seraph, I beg of you."

He was again about to refuse, but she held his mouth shut with a hand soft and smooth as satin.

7

"Do not say no. Let me at least have the pleasure of hoping you will come. And now it is your turn to kiss me, monsieur, in return for all the kisses I have given you."

Fresh, rosy, smiling lips which offer themselves to ours are never so tempting as when we are longing to kiss others but cannot.

Seraph looked a moment at Barbara, then pressed her closely to him and covered her lips with kisses.

"Serpent," he muttered between his teeth.

"Oh, in paradise the serpent always lurks," she returned laughingly. "Adieu," and she was gone.

Directly after, a britscha (light Polish carriage) drove into the court-yard; from it descended Pastor Zepharowitsch, his mighty better half, and son and daughter. While Luka was showing them into the drawing-room, Magdalina came flying up to where Seraph was seated, to tell him of their arrival.

"Milena is with them? Do you know her?"

"Yes."

"And do you not think her beautiful?"

"I only think one person beautiful."

"The lady who rode past us last evening on our way home?"

"The least of all."

"Whom, then?"

"Some one else."

"Ah, it is a secret, then. How provoking of you to have a secret!" and she was off again as quickly as she had come. "I know a pretty song," she called back over her shoulder to Seraph.

"What is it?"

Magdalina sang:

> "Mit dem Krebse tanzt der Fisch,
> Mit der Gans der Flederwisch."

"Oh, I know that song too," said Seraph laughingly, and they walked toward the castle singing like two happy, careless children the old song they had first heard and learned in their nurseries.

The Zepharowitsches remained to dinner at the castle. At dinner, the pastor entangled Emilian in a web of controversial discussion that lasted through the whole repast. A leaden weariness, in consequence, fell upon the others. The girls shyly pulled each other's frocks or tweaked at each other's long braids of hair.

Seraph and his friend exchanged remarks and witticisms through the medium of their note-books, which they passed from one to another under the shelter of the table-cloth.

Madame Zepharowitsch gave her whole attention to the dishes before her. At the dessert, however, there came a diversion. Seraph, who had been secretly instructed beforehand by the younger Zepharowitsch, now arose, and falling on his knees before Magdalina, before she could prevent him, he drew off one of her little satin slippers; handing it to Zepharowitsch, the latter filled it with champagne and returned it to Seraph, who, still kneeling, drank the wine from out of the shoe at a draught.

Every one at the table knew the significance of this act of true Polish homage. The elder people applauded, the younger smiled. Only Magdalina sat there with downcast eyes and burning cheeks, one hand nervously clutching the edge of the table.

"Allow me, gracious lady," Seraph begged, "to put the slipper on again."

"No," she replied harshly, and as though awaking from a dream, she tore the slipper out of his hand and ran quickly out of the room.

All present were astonished at her behavior, while Seraph, looking very pale and shocked, slowly arose from his knees. "What have I done?" he thought. "I thought she knew that I loved her. I had begun to hope she loved me in return."

They left the dining-room and returned to the drawing-room. Madame Zepharowitsch nodded in her chair; her husband and Emilian retired to the library; Seraph, Milena, and her brother went into the garden. Magdalina, however, did not make her appearance again; not even when the pastor's family drove off, and Seraph, mounting his horse, accompanied them on their way home. On his return he went out into the garden, hoping to find Magdalina there. Looking upward, he saw a figure leaning pensively against the turret of the tower. It was not

Magdalina's, however; the moonlight shone upon the pale, sad face of Emilian. Presently another shape appeared at his side. This time it was Magdalina. Seraph's heart throbbed violently as he looked upon her. She came up to Emilian, who had not until that moment perceived her, and clasped her arms tenderly about him. He drew her closer to him and kissed her. They stood so entwined, looking out before them down into the valley bathed in moonlight. The æolian harp above their heads filled the air with its wailing, yearning tones.

"So that is why she scorned me and refused my homage this evening," thought Seraph, his heart swelling hotly as he looked. "She loves him and he returns her love. It is time that I should leave this place."

He turned away sadly and seated himself on the bench beneath the linden tree. It was the place where he had been sitting when Barbara came to him. He leaned his head against the tree and sat there sunk in gloomy thought. Suddenly he arose. The desire to see Magdalina as she passed through the garden had taken possession of him. He placed himself at the fountain to await her coming, throwing one arm around the white neck of a marble nymph.

Magdalina came walking toward him. When she saw him, she started violently and ran past him quickly into the house. Seraph stood there looking after her.

"Blockhead," he muttered between his clinched teeth, "do you want any further proof of her dislike of you? Women—there is not one of them to be trusted. Emilian's wife was not an exception, but like all the rest of her sisterhood. What was it he said to you when you last talked together? It is better to study from the page of another's book of experience than to learn from our own. One pays for one's lessons with one's heart's drops. I am learning now and paying for my lesson."

He threw himself down by the basin of the fountain, and it seemed to him as though the statue of the nymph looked down scornfully upon him and with a smile of contempt on her marble lips.

Early the next morning Seraph mounted his horse and rode off in the direction of Sorpa, the home of the Countess Barvaroska.

He would see Barbara, would see if her love would not console for the mortification, the humiliation he had endured at Magdalina's hands. In her arms, with her lips pressed against his own, his heart might perhaps cease to ache for another.

As he rode up, he found the huntsmen and keepers already assembled in the court-yard. The dogs, coupled together, were straining in the leash and barking, in their impatience to be off. Grooms were leading horses, saddled and bridled, slowly up and down. Seraph sprang off his horse, and giving it in charge of the groom entered the door, which stood wide open. A pretty maid-servant came forward to meet him.

"Madame Trendaloska?" he inquired.

"This way, please," returned the abigail, tripping on before him.

At the end of the long corridor she stopped and pointed to a door, before which a large greyhound was lying.

Seraph knocked gently.

"Who is there?" inquired a voice from within—Barbara's.

"I, Barbara."

"But I don't know who ' I ' is."

"Seraph."

The door was opened directly, and Barbara appeared in it, clad in a dressing-gown, with her long, fair hair hanging loose upon her shoulders.

"You may kiss my hand," she said, extending it, "but then you must go away until I have put on my habit."

Seraph seized not one but both her little hands, and covered them with kisses; taking her in his arms, he put aside her hair and kissed her on her throat just below the little rosy ear.

"What are you doing?" exclaimed Madame Trendaloska, pushing him away from her. "Go, go," she added, and closed the door upon him, laughing. He heard the key turn in the lock as he stood there a moment gazing blankly at the door.

He went out into the court-yard again.

The hunting-party with the exception of Barbara was already there. It was some moments before she appeared, looking radiant and apologizing gayly for her delay. Seraph sprang forward to assist her to mount. The fanfare resounded, the party rode away. Their route lay through a small village, out on a road where a large wooden crucifix stood at the fork where two roads branched off, one to the right, the other to the left. The voices of the dogs were now uplifted loudly. A hare came in sight running across a meadow lying at the side of the road to the right; directly afterward a fox came trotting out from the wood at the left, paused to gaze a moment at the hunters, then ran rapidly along the edge of the road in the direction of a swamp which stretched itself out some furlongs off. The hunting-party was at once divided, some following the fox while the others gave chase to the hare.

Seraph found himself with Madame Trendaloska with those in pursuit of the hare. On horseback, Barbara was in her true element. Her slender but rather square and

angular figure looked its best in the close-
fitting habit of black cloth she wore. She
carried herself with ease and grace; her seat
in the saddle was perfection. It was she
who led the party. Seraph's looks hung
admiringly, half-disapprovingly, upon this
beautiful, daring, cruel creature. Strange
fancies flitted through his brain as he rode by
her side. He was reminded of that Amazo-
nian queen who dipped the head of the Per-
sian king, her faithless lover, beheaded by her
orders, into the blood which flowed from the
trunk from which it had just been severed;
of the Grand-duchess Olga, who ordered a
hundred knights, made captive in battle some
months before, to be slain on her marriage-
day. Suddenly, it seemed to his excited
fancy as if he had been transformed into
the horse on which Barbara was riding. He
was urged on and on by the cruel strokes of
her whip, in the pursuit of the flying hare.
He awoke suddenly from his dream, to hear
Barbara's exulting voice proclaiming the
death of the hare, to see her steel-blue eyes
glittering brightly with triumph, as the cav-

alcade of hunters surrounded her, with compliments and congratulations on her prowess. Then, wheeling his horse round suddenly, he set off at a gallop in the direction of Honoriec.

It was noon when he arrived there. He went directly up to his chamber, changed his hunting-suit, and descended the stairs. No one was to be seen in the drawing-rooms. He passed out of the door and stood at the top of the broad stone steps, looking around him.

The sun shone down brightly from a sky unflecked by the smallest cloud; the court-yard seemed to steam with heat.

The stones of the moat glistened in the sun's rays. Stillness reigned over all. The great wolf-hound had deserted his usual post before the door, and sought shelter beneath the shadow of the marble nymph at the fountain. Even the birds had hidden themselves among the cool shade of the branches and left off singing. On the broad, flat, mossy stones of the wall, and in the crevices of the stones of the court-yard, bright green lizards, and small brown snakes lay basking in the sun.

It was too hot to remain outside, Seraph decided, and sought shelter in the cool dark library. The coolness, the darkness were grateful to his eyes, half-blinded by the glare of the sun.

He threw himself languidly down upon a couch placed against the side of the wall, and lying there with half-shut lids, contemplated lazily some small floating particles of dust dancing in a ray of light which had stolen into the room through a crevice in the blind. "They are the souls of the letters," he murmured under his breath, "which have escaped from their confinement within the books and are dancing for joy at gaining their liberty." Lying there, he heard a sound as of somebody softly singing near him; looking around, however, he saw no one. The song died away presently. After a pause the Ariel-like melody began again. The books which filled the niche where he was lying were now thrown on to the floor suddenly, and with a laugh Magdalina appeared in the opening. She wore a gown of some soft, white filmy stuff, and a white veil was wound fantastically around her dark hair. It seemed to Seraph as though one of the dim, pale engravings in one of the great old folios had suddenly grown large, become alive, and stepped out from its place on the page.

"What are you doing here in my do·main?" she inquired, evidently surprised to find him there. "Do you not know," she went on laughingly, "that I have it in my power to punish you for your audacity?"

"I did not know," Seraph replied, gravely rising from the couch where he had thrown himself. "I will no longer intrude upon you."

"Stay." She interrupted him with a haughty gesture and a look of command. "I command you to remain here." Then breaking out into a laugh she continued: "Do you not know I am a witch, an en-chanter, and if you displease or disobey me, I have power immediately to change you into a moth or book-worm as a punishment

for your disobedience? Think of it, and
tremble. You would then be obliged to pass
your life between the covers of some books,
or in fluttering from one musty leather-covered volume to the other." ✓

"I can readily believe that you are a witch,
an enchantress. Have I not from the first
moment I saw you been the victim of your
spells? But let me warn you, mademoiselle,
that if you transform me into a moth, I
shall immediately fly to and hide myself in
the fur on your kazabaika [jacket], there to
remain. Cannot you transform me at once?
Think how delightful it would be to nestle
against your neck or tickle your cheek with
my wings."

"A blow from my hand would crush you
to death in an instant."

"What a delightful death that would be!
Pray, mademoiselle, wave your wand and
change me into a moth at once."

"Oh, if you desire a blow I can give it to
you without taking the trouble of trans-
forming you"—a light stroke of her hand
on Seraph's cheek accompanied her words.

"You are no longer displeased with me?" Seraph asked eagerly.

"Displeased with you? Why?"

"I feared I had vexed you yesterday evening at dinner."

"It was extremely impertinent of you, sir. I was very angry, indeed, with you *at the time.*"

"And Emilian, too, probably?"

"Emilian—angry, and at nonsense like that!"

"When a man loves a woman——"

"Emilian—in love—and with me! I am not a woman, I am only a girl." She began to laugh, spinning round and round the room in a quaint dance.

"Can you deny that you love him?"

"Deny it? of course not. I love him better than any one in the whole wide world. I should be the basest, the most ungrateful wretch alive if I did not love him." She paused and looked thoughtfully past him, then continued speaking in low, even tones, more as if soliloquizing than speaking to him: "I do not know if I ever had a moth-

er. I think I must have had one, for——"
Here Seraph could not refrain from smiling, but she went on unheeding: "It is all
dim and misty in my memory; but as in
a dream I can recall the shape of a tall,
beautiful woman. Sometimes she is on
horseback, and smiles down on my small
self looking up at her. Then she appears
to me dressed in purple and ermine, like
a queen. Then she is gone, and it is I who
am on horseback, and on the saddle-bow in
front of me sits a grinning, chattering ape.
That too vanishes, and I am in a great
drawing-room with marble pillars; from the
walls great pictures look down on me curiously. I pass through a long corridor; I hear
the sound of my uncertain footsteps as they
tread upon the marble floor; a great door is
opened by a liveried servant, and I am in a
large room with rows and rows of books
lining the walls, reaching almost up to the
vaulted ceiling. Through the open casement I look up at the shining stars, and then
a tall man, with a grave, kind face, stoops
and lifts me up upon his knee and speaks

8

to me, a little, trembling, forlorn child,
in tones as sweet and tender as the beautiful lady used. I have lost her—hardly her
memory remains; but he, thank God, is with
me still—has been always with me since the
night I, a little, little child, sitting on his
knee, looked up into his face and loved it.
And now, sir," turning proudly toward
Seraph, "perhaps you can give me a reason
for my not loving him." And before Seraph,
ashamed, remorseful, could stammer out a
word in extenuation, could ask pardon for
his unjust suspicions, she was gone.

CHAPTER VI

THE weather grew hotter and hotter. The windows of the chapel were glowing, sparkling in the rays of the midsummer sun. All vegetation was parched and dried up; a heavy mist hung pall-like upon the mountain tops and in the valley beneath. The parched earth longed and thirsted for rain. Seraph was sitting half-asleep on a bench in the garden, when he saw Magdalina come out of the house and cross the court-yard in the direction of the chapel. He sprang up and followed her. The coolness, the darkness of the chapel were grateful to his eyes, dazzled by the glare and heat outside. But Magdalina was nowhere to be seen—neither kneeling before the altar nor hidden away in the recesses of the dim organ-loft. After diligent search he was about to leave the chapel, when he heard his name called softly, and Magdalina's bright, fresh face and laughing eyes looked at him from out the railed window of a confessional box.

"What are you doing there?" he asked in astonishment.

"I am waiting for you," she returned calmly.

"For me?"

"Yes—for you—you. Sinner that you are, I am here to listen to your confession of your sins."

"What am I to confess?"

"Kneel down, first; one always does at confession."

Seraph knelt. His face, as he knelt, was on a level with hers, and only separated from it by the lattice of the window. "What do you want me to confess?" he asked, looking straight into her eyes.

Hers fell a moment, then plucking up courage she raised them again and went on laughingly: "You are to answer truthfully any and all questions I may put to you."

"Ask, and I will answer."

"Truthfully?"

L

"Of course."

"On your honor?"

"On my honor."

"Then tell me who it is you are in love with, Monsieur Seraph — Milena or the Countess Barbara?"

"With neither. I love you, Magdalina."

"Oh, you promised me to tell me the truth."

"I am telling you the truth. I love you, and you only."

The lovely face of the young girl had now approached quite near to the lattice; his own was pressed close up against it.

"You are joking. I am sure you are laughing at me in your sleeve."

"I swear I am not. I love you. Shall I say it again and again? I love you—I love you—I love you."

"Oh!" she murmured, blushing rosy as a flame, "can it be true?" Then followed a pause, broken only by the quickened breathing of those two young, passionate creatures, and the ticking of a wood-worm in the panels of the confessional.

"And you—do you love me?" Seraph asked, breaking the silence suddenly. For answer, her small white fingers drew back the lattice and a bright face looked down smilingly at him.

The chapel-door now swung open on its creaking hinges, and Seraph, jumping to his feet, saw a tall, black-robed woman, thickly veiled, approaching him. Two large, brilliant eyes glared on him from behind the meshes of the veil, and a sharp, stern voice said: "Seraph, what are you doing here?"

Magdalina, frightened by the sudden and unexpected apparition, had drawn the lattice down and hidden herself within the confessional box.

"Mother," he stammered, "what has brought you here?"

Stefanida sank down on one of the benches and threw back her veil. "Who was that girl?" she inquired sternly. Seraph remained silent. "And for this girl, for her," she went on bitterly, "you have forgotten your vow to me—the solemn oath you swore to me."

"I have forgotten nothing—nothing, mother," Seraph answered firmly, "but it is not you, mother, who should reproach me, but I you. You have deceived me—cruelly —wickedly."

"How have I deceived you?"

"You have slandered, cruelly maligned the best, the kindest man in the world. There is not one syllable of truth in your accusations against Emilian."

His mother broke out into a short, bitter laugh.

"Oh, I see! He has woven his web around you——"

"Emilian—he is incapable of deceiving, of ensnaring any one. How can you imagine——"

"But this girl—what is she to him?"

"That girl is his daughter—rescued by him from poverty, from ill-usage, and adopted by him as his child."

"You are in love with this girl, his tool," she interrupted him violently, "and your passion for her has made you a traitor to me—to your mother. Do you not see that this creature is only an instrument in the hands of Emilian?"

"No, no, no!" answered Seraph indig-nantly. "This child, so sweet, so inno-cent——"

"This child, so sweet, so innocent, is the decoy with which Emilian has caught you in his toils. Are you blind? Can you not see that she will ruin you? Has she not caused you already to forget your oath and the purpose which brought you here? She is his tool and a trap set by him for your destruction."

"Ridiculous!".

"We shall see," returned his mother, ris-ing and standing before him, her whole fig-ure shaking with passion.

"Be honest, mother, and answer me one question," said Seraph, seizing her by the wrist. "Were you, mother—how can I say it?—but were you ever—this man—Emilian —whom you hate so terribly, whom you long to see lying dead at your feet—what were you once to him?"

"Nothing."

"Then what great injury can he have done you? What wrong that merits a revenge so pitiless—so terrible? Mother! you MUST answer me this question."

"I never shall."

"Then I am absolved, released from my oath. I refuse to be a blind instrument in the hands of a cruel, vindictive woman."

Stefanida gazed at him a moment with wide-opened eyes, then began to laugh horribly—the laugh of a demon. So laughing, she left the chapel and passed out through the court-yard.

Emilian stood on the steps of the castle as she went by. He beckoned to Luka, who was standing by the gate, to come to him. "Did you see that lady?" he whispered. The old servant nodded silently—solemnly. Emilian muttered half under his breath, "Demons and spirits of the lower world walking about in the full light of day. What can they portend?"

At dinner there were guests present from Lemberg. Seraph sat silent, eating little,

but swallowing glass after glass of fiery
Hungarian wine. His glances rested tenderly on Magdalina, who smiled and reddened under his gaze. When the guests
were assembled in the drawing-room, she
came up to the dark corner where he had
ensconced himself. "What is the matter
with you?" she inquired. "Why have you
hidden yourself away? And that woman
with whom you were speaking in the chapel,
who was she?"

"A friend of my mother's."

"You are not telling me the truth, Seraph,
I fear. As well as I could see her through
her veil, and I saw her eyes—her bright,
wicked, cruel eyes—quite plainly, she resembles a portrait here in the castle. Only
the woman in the picture is very much
younger than this one."

"Are you certain of what you are saying?
One often sees resemblances where they do
not exist in fact——"

"I am quite certain," she returned, "that
the lady I saw to-day resembles a picture
hanging up in one of the rooms here."

"Where is the picture? Could I see it?"

"It hangs in one of the disused rooms in the second story in the wing which is always kept closed."

"Who occupied those rooms formerly? Do you know?"

"Indeed I do not. Luka will never tell me."

Seraph remained deep in thought a few moments; then rousing himself, he said suddenly: "It is not possible that you could deceive—betray me?"

"I do not know what you mean," she answered, looking wonderingly at him; then pointing to a bracelet in the shape of a serpent which she wore on her wrist, she continued: "Look, Seraph: the serpent, you know, is an emblem of eternity—without beginning, without end. I think my love for you is like that."

Seraph raised her hand and put it a moment to his lips. "Could you," he said after a moment's thought, "could you show me the portrait that you speak of?"

"I will see if I can find the key to the

room. For you I would do anything." She gave a quick glance in the direction where Emilian was seated, then glided swiftly out of the room.

Seraph remained half-hidden in the obscurity of the corner he had chosen; from there he gazed long and searchingly at Emilian. "No," he said to himself, turning his eyes away after an inspection of some minutes, "a man whose countenance, whose every look denotes his goodness, whose face is a mirror of high and noble thoughts, cannot be the fiend my mother has depicted. If he is false, language possesses no word strong enough to brand his hypocrisy. But he is not false."

Looking up, he saw Magdalina in the door, half-concealed by the portière, beckoning to him. He got up and followed her. As he entered the corridor she slipped her hand into his and led him along to the staircase leading up to the second story. They ascended, and, entering an upper gallery, they came to a small corridor, at the end of which a deep embrasure in the wall appeared, shut off in its turn by a white-and-gold door. Magdalina opened this door with a key she carried, and they entered another corridor into which an antechamber opened. Adjoining the antechamber was a small boudoir. The doors all stood open, revealing a small suit of apartments, faintly lighted up by the moonlight which had found its way through interstices of the closed blinds. Magdalina lighted the wax-lights in a branched candlestick standing on the chimney-piece. Seraph stood gazing blankly around him.

"What is the matter with you, Seraph?" Magdalina asked anxiously.

"I cannot explain it," he returned, "but such a strange feeling has taken possession of me. As I stand here, I seem to hear music, the music of an old song; but I do not know what it is, the melody, or recall when or where it was that I heard it. But it is in the air all around and about me." He stood as though listening. Magdalina, with a look of alarm, hastily drew back a curtain hanging before one of the doors.

"Here is the drawing-room."

Seraph took a step forward and looked in through the door. The furniture was covered with yellow damask, with large white birds embossed upon it; on the wall pictures were hanging. Two seemed familiar to Seraph: one, a large landscape, a forest, with a still blue lake in the foreground, through which a mounted herdsman was driving a herd of plunging horses and cattle; the other represented a Venetian palace with its small canal on which a gondola floated.

"My God!" he muttered half under his breath; "this room—these pictures—where have I ever seen them before?"

"Seraph, how odd you behave, how strange you look! You frighten me."

"I have been in these rooms before. But when—I have quite forgotten. When——"

"In a dream, perhaps."

"Impossible."

He entered the adjoining room. Here the furniture was covered with gay Turkish damask; a little inlaid writing-desk stood in a recess in a window. On the top stood a

Dresden china statuette representing Polish and Turkish cavalry in combat. Before the fireplace was a low divan; an embroidered satin pillow lay upon it, a bearskin rug was stretched before it. Seraph's head reeled as he gazed about him. There was a little painted fire-screen on which the battle of Navarino was portrayed. How often had he gazed at these ships with their cannons belching fire and smoke! His head must have then been on a level with the top of the screen, he told himself.

"I know this room!" he exclaimed loudly and suddenly. "I have often been in it." He stepped hastily into the last room of the suit. It was furnished as a bedchamber; the bed with its white canopy, its silken counterpane thrown carelessly aside, as if the occupant had but just arisen from it. Before the bed stood a pair of small satin slippers; across the back of a chair a jacket of rose-colored satin, bordered and lined with sable, was lying. He recognized this jacket, out of which a swarm of moths flew as he took it up in his hands. On the chimney-piece stood a little marble clock; a loop of faded pink ribbon hung down on one side of it. On Seraph's pulling on the loop the clock began at once to play a little, tinkling tune.

Ah, that tune! It was the same which had been ringing in his ears from the very first moment he entered these rooms.

It was a mazourka, to the music of which the hero, General Chlopicki, had written the words of his famous battle-song. This song—who was it who had sung it again and again to Seraph as he lay, a child, in her arms?

Who, indeed, if not his mother?

And there, illumined by the moonlight flooding the chamber, Magdalina having just drawn the blind, there over the chimney-piece hung her portrait—her portrait, when young and beautiful and happy. That was her perfect figure, slender, round, and supple, depicted on the canvas, and her bright, smiling, yet cold eyes looking out from it. Cruel eyes, Magdalina had called them. The figure in the picture was clad

in a white dress over which a velvet, fur-
trimmed jacket was worn. The original of
the jacket still hung across the chair. On
the breast of the jacket in the portrait a red
rose was pinned. Seraph stood there gazing
as if in a dream. He was quite unconscious
that Magdalina, frightened at the strange-
ness of his looks, was calling to him.

His mother had told him the truth, then.
Emilian had deceived, betrayed, and then
forsaken her—betrayed her as he had done
Magdalina, who in her turn would be aban-
doned, forsaken. His mother was right:
the girl standing at his side was Emilian's
tool.

She would lure the son to his ruin as he,
Emilian, had lured the mother.

His blood was boiling, his head whirling,
as he stood there gazing in silence on his
mother's portrait. A hoarse oath burst
from his white, trembling lips. Pushing
Magdalina roughly aside, he hurried from
the apartment.

Emilian was in the little drawing-room
with his guests when Seraph, pale, with

9

wildly flashing eyes, rushed in and stood there confronting him.

"What has happened?" Emilian asked, alarmed at the wild aspect of the young man.

"You have lied to me!" answered the other through his clinched teeth. "You are a villain! My mother was right when she called you one."

"Your mother! Young man," returned Emilian in quiet, firm tones, "I have told you again and again that I do not know your mother."

"Then you lied to me," retorted Seraph violently. No longer able to control himself, he raised his hand as though to strike Emilian to the ground.

One of the guests at that moment, however, threw himself before Emilian, while Magdalina caught hold of Seraph's upraised arm.

"I demand the satisfaction usual between gentlemen," Seraph continued, letting his arm drop heavily at his side.

"Sir," returned Emilian, "I suppose you

will not refuse first to tell me the reason of this extraordinary behavior on your part?"

"I refuse all and any explanation. I desire from you only the satisfaction usual between gentlemen."

"Very well," returned Emilian quietly, "and now for the present the matter can rest." He reseated himself on the sofa and resumed the conversation with his guests so unceremoniously interrupted.

Seraph quitted the room without one glance in the direction of Magdalina, who, half-fainting from terror, had fallen into an arm-chair near the window-recess. In the court-yard he found Luka, and ordered him to have his horse saddled and brought round to him immediately; mounted it and set off at a gallop toward Wislonka, the village where his friend Zepharowitsch lived. That same evening Zepharowitsch came to Honoriec, and he and Count Fredro, the guest who had flung himself between Emilian and Seraph, arranged for a duel early the next morning.

After the guests and Zepharowitsch had

departed Emilian retired to his study,
where a light might have been seen burning
until the morning. He had much to do.
He must put his affairs in order. In those
hours he bade adieu to life and calmly pre-
pared for death. The task was not a difficult one; he was "aweary o' the sun."
When he had finished arranging his papers
and had written directions concerning what
he wished done after his death, he leaned
back in the chair, his head falling on his
breast. He looked backward on his past
life as a master of a vessel wrecked on an
inhospitable shore looks back on his sinking
ship.

Hope, happiness—he had done with them
years before. It was an easy task for him
to prepare to meet death with courage, with
resignation.

But it was different with Seraph. He
was young, and till now had known no
sorrow. Hope had only just spread her
bright wings and flown away from his side.

It was with him as though he stood before a door over which a thick, dark cur-

tain hung covered with strange hieroglyph-
ics. By to-morrow, probably, the curtain
would be lifted, the door closed after him.

He was a prey to nervous terrors against
which he fought in vain.

He wrote letters to his mother, to Magdalina; strange to say, last of all, a letter of
affectionate adieu to Barbara. When he
had finished the night was done, the dawn
had arrived. He went out into the garden;
the stars had grown dim and the birds
were stirring among the leaves. The day
was breaking when Seraph and Zepharowitsch mounted their horses and rode off to
the place chosen for the meeting. The ren-
dezvous was the meadow in the forest
where Seraph had walked with Emilian and
Magdalina. They were the first to arrive.
They dismounted, tied their horses to a tree,
and threw themselves down on the grass to
await the arrival of the others. All around
them was peace. The sun had arisen and
was strewing rays of golden light among
the dark foliage of the fir trees. The birds
sang and flew hither and thither around

above them. A squirrel ran up into the tree beneath which they had thrown themselves and threw a pine-cone mischievously down upon them. But Seraph saw and heard nothing of the beauty, the mirth around him. He heard nothing but the monotonous sound of a woodpecker in the tree above him. It sounded in his ears like the driving of nails in his coffin.

A light carriage was driven rapidly toward them. It drew up a short distance off, and Emilian, the count, and a surgeon got out of it. Zepharowitsch, raising his hat courteously, went forward to consult with the count. A few words were exchanged; the ground measured; the pistols examined and loaded.

A moment later the opponents stood facing each other, both apparently calm, but Seraph a prey to indescribable and secret agitation.

From the moment that his fingers closed upon the pistol, a feeling as if he were about to commit a great, a horrible crime— a murder, sacrilegious in the extreme—had taken possession of his soul. The sun itself seemed to hide its face in horror at the deed he was about to commit.

The sign was given and the adversaries slowly approached each other; two shots resounded, almost at the same instant.

A moment both stood upright, the smoking pistols clasped in their hands; the next Seraph staggered, reeled, and fell, face downward, to the ground. The blood gushed from a wound in his side and crimsoned the green turf where he lay.

CHAPTER VII.

WHEN Seraph again opened his eyes and looked wonderingly around him, he discovered that he was lying in his own bed in the same room he had occupied since his arrival at Honoriec.

Had he dreamed — a horrid, painful dream? He turned uneasily in the bed, and as he did so his wound pained him. Then he knew it was no dream, but reality. But if he and Emilian had fought, how was it that he was again at the castle? His head grew dizzy as he turned the problem over in his brain, as though he saw in a mist the figures of Luka, Emilian, and Magdalina at his bedside. Then he again lost consciousness.

When he awoke, the sunlight was pouring in through the open blinds of his chamber; outside the tall trees rustled and the

finches sang merrily among the branches.
Magdalina sat at his bedside, pale, with
woful, dark eyes. She caught his look
resting on her, smiled faintly, and rising
from the chair where she was sitting, she
bent over and asked anxiously: "You are
better, are you not?"

"Very much," he returned, looking around
the room wonderingly.

"Will you not drink?"

"Not now." He reached out his hand
and caught hold of Magdalina's. "Have I
dreamed, or was I really wounded by——"
Then, without waiting for an answer, "Do
you love me?" he asked anxiously.

"Ah, with all my heart, with all my
soul!"

"How good, how kind you are! And you
find it possible to forgive me?"

From that day the fever abated and he
recovered rapidly.

On Seraph seemed to have descended the
peace, the unquestioning faith of a little
child. He slept, ate, played dominoes with
Magdalina, or chatted long hours with her.

He never mentioned his mother or Emilian. The events of the few past weeks—the duel, his wound, his anger toward Emilian, his distrust of Magdalina—had vanished utterly. With the help of Luka he began to walk about his chamber; finally he was able to descend the stair and walk in the garden.

There, resting in his favorite spot in the shadow of the lime-tree, he would sit listening to the buzzing of the bees, the songs of the thrushes, or would watch Magdalina flitting in her bright-colored frock among the flower-beds. Once he called to her and asked her anxiously: "Has my mother been here?"

"No," she answered softly.

"And Emilian, why does he keep away from me?"

"He spent hours at your bedside while you were unconscious; since then, however, he has kept away, fearing you would not care to see him."

"I would like to see him. Please ask him to come to me."

Some hours later, when Seraph had returned to his chamber, Magdalina came into the study where Emilian was sitting.

"He has asked to see you," she said.

"If I could only guess what it was that made him attack me so suddenly," said Emilian thoughtfully—"what can have set him against me so. Do you know?"

"It must have been his mother."

"His mother? Who is she? A certain Madame Temkin, a woman quite unknown to me. He must have become suddenly insane. But no, he seems quite rational. Though, after all, his sudden furious attack on me that evening after dinner certainly looked like madness."

Magdalina returned with a timid look and in low, hesitating tones: "There was a woman who came to see him on the day before your duel."

"A woman! The one who went through the court-yard?"

"The same. I think she is his mother."

"His mother—that woman? Impossible!" He sprang from his chair and walked quickly up and down the room.

"I am sure it was his mother, though he told me, when I asked him who it was, that it was a friend of his mother's."

"That is more likely. But I must see him. I must unravel this mystery. Come, we will go to him."

"Now—at this hour?"

"I can wait no longer. I must speak to him."

"Let me go to him first and prepare him for your coming."

When Emilian entered Seraph's chamber, he found him lying in bed, propped up by pillows. He hesitated on the threshold, but Seraph turning toward him with a smile and outstretched hand, he came quickly up to the bedside and grasped the proffered hand.

"So we are friends again, I hope, and shall be friends forever. But that in future no further misunderstanding may arise between us, I must ask you to explain some things which, as yet, are not quite clear to me. Pray tell me why you spoke the words you did to me the evening before our meeting—words that I have forgiven, but I fear I can never forget? I am even at this moment quite ignorant why we fought."

"From the first moment I saw you," returned Seraph in trembling tones, "I respected, admired you, revered you; our further intercourse caused these feelings of respect and admiration to ripen into affection, sincere and true affection on my part. Judge what a revulsion of feeling I experienced to learn that the man I revered and loved beyond any other being in the world had deceived me—cruelly, deliberately deceived me."

"I deceived you? And how, may I ask?"

"You assured me on your honor that you were quite unacquainted with my mother, had never even heard her name, and yet you do know her, have——"

"I swear to you——"

"Do not swear."

"By everything that is holy, I swear to you that I have no acquaintance with any woman of the name of Temkin."

"Then you knew her under another name. I no longer believe her accusations against you, but that you know, or have known, my mother, and intimately, I am sure. I made the discovery the evening before the duel."

"What do you mean?"

"I mean that on that evening I saw my mother's portrait hanging in one of the disused rooms of the wing in the second story."

"My wife's portrait," returned Emilian softly.

"Then my mother was your wife," returned the young man, his lips white and quivering.

"Seraph," returned Emilian, very much agitated, "do you not remember once being called by another name—a long time ago when you were little? Think, try and recollect, I implore you."

"Was I ever called by another name?" replied Seraph slowly and thoughtfully. "Let me see—when I used to hear the clock on the chimney-piece play the old tune every day, and my mother sat in the room before her embroidery-frame, while I lay upon the bear-skin rug at her feet—what name was it she called me by? I cannot remember what it was. I can remember tumbling over a great, shaggy dog which had followed a tall man into the room—a tall man, with a grave, kind face, who carried a gun in one hand and a fox he had just killed in the other; he looks down at me and smiles and calls me— My God! what name is it that he calls me by? He calls me—ah, I have it now!—he calls me ' *Wladin.*' "

"And your mother's name?" interrupted Emilian, trembling.

" Is Stefanida."

He bent over the bed and gathered the young man closely to his heart, while the tears fell on his head like rain. " My God!" he murmured, "I thank thee. It is my son—my long-lost son."

They held each other, clasped in a close embrace; then Seraph gently freed himself from his father's arms, and looking up at him whispered remorsefully: "And I—God forgive me!—might have killed you."

"And I did nearly kill you," returned Emilian. Again they were silent, holding each other tightly by the hand.

Suddenly Seraph, raising his head, whispered half under his breath: "Magdalina—is she my sister?"

"No," returned Emilian, smiling indulgently down at him; "there is no obstacle to your marrying each other. Believe me, I have long known of your love for her and that this love of yours was returned."

"Who were her parents?" asked Seraph eagerly.

"I do not know. I was a lonely man—I had no longer wife nor child. One day a circus-rider came to me, bringing the child with her, and offered to sell me the little one. As I stood there talking to the woman, the child crept close up to me and caught hold of my hand in both her tiny ones, looking up entreatingly into my face with her great, dark eyes. From that moment I loved her and determined never to send her away. The woman assured me that the child's parents were dead. I do not know,

of course, but I have often thought she had
been stolen by the circus-riders from her
home. I bought the little one from them,
however, and ever since she has been like
my own daughter to me—a dutiful, loving
daughter. She has been my pupil, too. I
have taught her to love truth and nature
and to enjoy solitude. She has a heart of
gold and a temper sweet as summer flowers.
I am happy to think you have won for
your own this heart so true, so gener-
ous, so loving." He left the room a moment, returning, however, directly after
with Magdalina. Taking Seraph's hand he
placed the girl's hand in it. "You are
mine now," he said, "both mine, my dear
children, and you must not leave me. For
me, life with its hopes, its joys, is finished.
My happiness will consist in beholding the
happiness of those about me—of those I love.
I shall live only for you and in you, my dear
son and daughter."

When Seraph awoke the next morning,
he beheld Luka on his knees at the bedside.
He was weeping.

10

"What has happened, Luka?" he inquired anxiously.

"Oh, my dear young master," sobbed Luka, "I am weeping for joy to have you with us again. And to think that you were nearly killed by the old master! If he had killed you instead of only wounding you—O my God! my God! How far away seem those days when you sat on my knees and with your little hands pulled my mustache. But we have you again. One should praise God for that. But will not the gracious lady deign to come back to us again, and live here as she used? Pardon me, gracious master, my old tongue runs away with me sometimes."

Seraph laid his hand on Luka's shoulder. "Now, Luka, you want to tell me something. Out with it."

"I only wanted to tell you the gracious lady, your mother, is at Sentyn——"

"At the Countess'? How do you know, Luka?"

"The pretty peasant woman who came once to see you—you remember her—she came again while you were so ill, and she told me."

"That my mother was at Sentyn?"

"Yes, sir; she has been there a long time."

Seraph sprang out of bed, and with Luka's help dressed himself quickly. His heart was beating violently, his blood was flowing quickly through his veins; a hundred thoughts chased each other through his mind. He must leave the room, the house; he felt stifled. He must get out into the open air. Magdalina came forward to meet him as he descended the stairs and offered him her arm. He drew her to him and kissed her fondly, but declined the proffered arm. Strength had come to him in a moment. He had a duty to perform, and he must do it at once, and alone. He ordered Gedeon to harness the horses to a light carriage, then went into the house, where he found Emilian awaiting him anxiously.

"You are going out? Where?" he inquired.

"To Sentyn, to my mother."

Emilian looked at him earnestly, but spoke not a word. He and Magdalina, however, accompanied him to the carriage.

"When will you be back?" inquired Emilian hesitatingly. "To-day?"

"Surely."

Gedeon cracked his whip loudly, and the carriage rolled swiftly out of the court-yard.

Arrived at Sentyn, Seraph, unannounced, entered the room where his mother was seated alone.

She sat at the window opening out on the garden, and looking out at it. She had not heard Seraph enter. When he came close up to her chair she turned quickly, and seeing him, sprang up with a loud cry—the cry of a wounded bird of prey—and flung her arms about him. She did not speak a word, only held him, and held him as though she would never let him go, and all the time her tears streamed forth.

Seraph was alarmed at this display of emotion on her part. He had never before known her to weep.

After a while she seemed suddenly to

grow ashamed of her emotion. She released him abruptly, and returning to her seat she asked coldly, her head turned away from him: "Why did you come here?"

"To see you, to speak to you, mother," he returned, greatly moved. "I beg you to listen quietly to what I have to say to you," he continued, taking a seat opposite her. "I know everything," he said solemnly.

"What is it you know, Seraph? Tell me."

"I know that Emilian is my father and that you were his wife—his fondly loved wife."

His mother trembled violently, but no word came from over her white lips. A pause, a painful one, ensued.

"He told you that?" Stefanida asked at last. Her voice was hoarse, her bosom heaved violently.

"He told me the history of his life and yours, before he or I knew that I was his son. It was only yesterday that I learned he was my father; though I had learned long before that to love, to revere, to worship him. I must repeat his own words to you, mother, then you can judge how deeply you have sinned against him." And Seraph related all that Emilian had told him since his arrival at Honoriec.

His mother listened in silence and with averted head. She never looked at her son, but kept her gaze constantly fixed on the tall old trees outside the window.

When Seraph had finished speaking, there was again silence between them. Soon Seraph, however, left his seat, and going up to his mother, he bent over her, taking one of her hands in his. He spoke in a low, deep voice words that caused her to shudder and turn pale:

"Do you realize now, mother, what you have done? That you almost succeeded in making a parricide of your son? Had Emilian even been as guilty as you supposed, instead of being innocent of all injury toward you, what right had you to seek to revenge yourself on him—and through me, his child? It was the thought of a demon—of a lost, guilty soul—and not that of a woman."

Seraph felt his mother's hand growing cold

in his own as he spoke to her. With a sudden, impatient motion she snatched it away
from him, and throwing herself face downward among the cushions she began to weep
violently. Her whole frame was shaken by
the tempest of emotion. Seraph, despite
his youth, was not ignorant of the beneficent
power of tears. He divined that the ice
in which for so many years she had incased
her heart was melting. She would be best
alone, he thought, and turning left the room
quietly.

Hours went past and still he had received
no summons from his mother to return.
Evening was come, when he entered the
room again, to find her pacing restlessly up
and down, her arms clasped tightly across
her breast. She stood still when he entered,
and looked long and earnestly at him. Her
glance was high and proud as usual, but no
longer stern, no longer cruel.

"What must I do?" she asked him softly.
"What shall I do to obtain my husband's
forgiveness, his pardon? Alas! I can never
hope for his love again."

"You must return with me, and at once, to Emilian."

"Never! It is impossible."

"Mother, you must! Does not your own heart tell you that you must?"

"I cannot," she replied gloomily.

"Then farewell, mother. I shall never see you again. I shall never more call you by the sacred name of mother."

"Seraph!"

He turned away toward the door.

"Farewell, mother, and forever," he said brokenly.

"Stop!" She came slowly up to him and looked long and fixedly into his eyes. "Is he expecting me?" she asked softly.

"No."

"But if he should spurn me—refuse even to see me."

"He spurn you! he refuse to see—to pardon you! Mother, he is goodness—kindness itself. But, after all, do you deserve his pardon? Have you any right to complain if he repulses you? Remember how you have treated him—he who is the noblest, the best man in the world. The angels in heaven are no better than he, I think."

She trembled violently, her shaking limbs refused to hold her, and she dropped heavily into a chair near by and beckoned Seraph to approach her, whispering with white lips as he bent down to hear what she might say:

"Let us go to him at once. Order the carriage to be got ready."

"The carriage is ready. It has been standing in the court-yard since my arrival here."

"So much the better." She drew on a jacket of Turkish stuff which hung on the back of a chair near her, set a gold-embroidered baschlick on her fair hair, and taking her son's arm they left the room and descended to the court-yard. As she was about to put her foot on the carriage-step, Gedeon gave a loud cry and fell down on his knees.

"The gracious lady—the mistress!" he exclaimed, kissing the hem of her robe.

"Rise, old man," exclaimed Stefanida,

greatly moved. "Are you really so glad to see me?"

"Glad, gracious lady! God himself only knows how glad I am. For years I have prayed for this moment night and day——"

"Drive on!" exclaimed Seraph impatiently.

"Where to, young master?"

"To Honoriec."

Gedeon mounted the box quickly, cracked his whip loudly, and the horses set out on a gallop toward Honoriec.

During the drive mother and son exchanged no word; only sat there, hand clasped in hand.

It was a lovely night. The moon shone over all, in a seemingly jocund mood. On the short, dark, slender fir trees it had put white surplices, turning them into a procession of choir-boys. The lilies of the fields were clad in dresses of translucent, shimmering silver. A halo of light was drawn around the thorn-crowned, bowed-down head of the Saviour on the crucifix at the cross-road. On the chimneys of the

houses were set white night-caps, and on the
noses of the Turks which upheld the balcony
at the castle it had mischievously drawn
long white streaks. Over the shoulders of
the nymph at the fountain seemed a mantle
of lace fine as gossamer.

Hearing the carriage drive into the court-
yard, Luka came out of the door and down
the steps, and held the carriage-door open.
As he saw Seraph sitting there with his
mother he began to tremble violently, while
the tears streamed down his sunken,
wrinkled cheeks. "Ah, gracious lady," he
stammered, "but you have been long away
from us." Stefanida smiled sadly and held
out her hand to him. Magdalina now came
running down the steps, and taking her
hand, kissed it reverently.

Stefanida looked at her in silence a moment, then drew her to her breast and
kissed her affectionately. Seraph led the
way into the house. He went through the
long corridor leading to Emilian's study.
He knocked; then opening the door in response to a permission to enter, he held back

the curtains for his mother to enter the room, and closing the door softly he went away.

Emilian sat at his desk. He turned at the sound made by the rustling curtains. As he saw who it was standing there in the room alone with him, he made an effort to rise from his chair, but his trembling limbs refused their office. He bent down his head and covered his face with his shaking hands. Stefanida hastened to him and fell down on her knees at his feet. He bent down and, lifting her in his arms, he drew her to his heart. Silently they held each other there, clasped in a close embrace.

At last Emilian, freeing himself gently from his wife's arms and looking down at her, broke the silence. "Why did you hate me so bitterly?" he asked wonderingly.

"Because—I loved you so deeply and was jealous of you," she answered.

CHAPTER VIII

ORE than a year has gone by since Stefanida's return to her old home. Everything has changed since her advent there. Solitude, silence, have given way to innocent mirth.

Even the old trees no longer whisper sad, mysterious secrets to one another, but rustle their leaves gayly and really seem to laugh softly now and then.

The nymph at the fountain, coquette that she is, has a smile now for every new-comer.

The grim old wolf-hound has forgotten his dignity enough to make friends with an impertinent kitten, which now lies snugly curled up on his gray, shaggy back.

Luka has doffed his sombre suit of black, and goes about resplendent in a livery of sky-blue, with innumerable silver buttons bedecking it. He hums gay old songs beneath his breath all day long. Gedeon's red nose shines brightly between his twinkling eyes, a cheery beacon-fire.

In the wing where for so many years no ray of light was allowed to penetrate, all the windows and doors now stand wide open, letting in the cheerful light of day and the songs of the birds.

The swallows and sparrows have nested in every eave and niche about the building. But at this season the storks and swallows are away, have flown to the south, for the time of year is the autumn—autumn which has given its bright tints to tree and shrub, and during the night covers the grass, still green, with a white mantle of hoar-frost, and hangs twinkling diamonds on every branch and twig. The sparrows chatter louder than ever before. The sun still shines warmly in through door and window, for the sun, one knows, loves the sight of good and happy people.

Emilian is sitting at work before his desk, and only three steps away from him, in a chair in the window-recess, sits Stefanida.

She has on a kazabaika of pink satin trimmed and lined with sable, and sits working before her embroidery-frame.

The æolian harp plays now a cradle-song, for in the great chamber above, looking out on the garden, sits Magdalina, holding an infant in her arms.

And the man who stands there leaning over her chair, gazing down fondly at the mother and babe, is her husband, Seraph.